THE HEART REMEMBERS

SMALL TOWN SECOND CHANCE ROMANCE

PAPERBACK

SAVANNA SHAY

SAVANNA SHAY BOOKS

THE RETURN

Marcus

I pull my car to a stop just outside the **Welcome to Fairhope** sign, gripping the steering wheel like it's the only thing keeping me from turning the hell around.

Everything looks the same. The same lazy stretch of road, the same rusting sign, the same small-town smell of pine and coffee drifting in from Main Street. If I focus hard enough, I can almost hear the echo of my own past, the sound of my cleats pounding against the field, Annabelle's laugh slipping through the summer air.

But I don't let myself focus. I haven't let myself in years.

Instead, I take a slow breath, roll my shoulders back, and pull into town.

I know this is a mistake. Coming back here. But the thing is, mistakes and I have always had a thing for each other.

Main Street hasn't changed. The usual suspects are still around—the guys who never left, standing outside the gas station like it's their second home, the old-timers who still wear their high school varsity jackets even though their beer bellies are testing the seams. It's like stepping into a time machine.

And then I see her.

At first, I think I'm imagining it. A cruel trick my brain is playing. But no—she's real. Annabelle Dawson. She's sitting near the window in a small circle of sunlight, a mug clutched in both hands like it holds all the warmth in the world.

Her auburn hair's shorter than I remember—pulled back in a soft bun with loose strands escaping to frame her face. There's still that softness in her features, that quiet glow she always carried, even when she didn't know it.

She's wearing a pale blue sweater and jeans, something simple, but she still looks like the kind of beautiful that sneaks up on you. The kind you feel before you even know why.

For a second, I just sit there like an idiot, staring.

And then I see the wheelchair.

My chest tightens. Hard.

Annabelle. *In a wheelchair.*

I don't even realize I've parked until someone knocks on my window. I blink up and see Ethan Carter grinning at me like he just won the lottery.

"Well, well, if it isn't Marcus Gray," he says, shaking his head. "Did hell freeze over, or did you finally run out of places to disappear to?"

I snort, shoving the door open. "Thought I'd come back and see if this town still sucks."

Ethan laughs, pulling me into a quick hug before stepping back. "Oh, it does. It absolutely does." Then his grin dims a little. "You saw her, didn't you?"

I don't even have to ask who he's talking about. I just nod. "What happened?"

Ethan sighs, rubbing the back of his neck. "Car accident. A couple of years after you left. It was bad. She was in a coma for weeks. Woke up with memory loss and…" He jerks his head toward her. "She's been in that chair ever since."

My stomach twists. "She doesn't remember me?"

Ethan shakes his head. "Not even a little."

Not even a little.

I don't know why that stings as much as it does. It's not like we left things in some perfect, storybook ending. *I left.* I let her go. I told myself I had to after the injury that ended my dreams of being a star quarterback.

I couldn't stay here and rot. I had to get away… and I couldn't let a high school love story get in the way..

I glance at Ethan, who's watching me carefully. He was my best friend back in the day. The guy who always had my back, whether it was sneaking out of detention or covering for me when I was off doing something reckless. We were inseparable once, but I guess I left him behind, too. And yet, here he is, standing next to me like no time has passed at all.

My eyes dart toward Annabelle again. My stomach sinks to the floor when I take it in—she doesn't remember me at all.

I should walk away. She looks happy. I should let her be.

But I already know I won't.

Because I see it—the flickers in her expression, the way she pauses sometimes like she's reaching for something just out of grasp.

She might not remember me.

But I remember her.

And I think it's time I remind her who I am.

～

3

I can still hear the roar of the crowd.

It's deafening, vibrating in my chest, filling my veins with adrenaline. The stadium lights burn down from above, the crisp autumn air biting at my exposed skin. Sweat drips down my temple, but I don't feel it. Not when I'm this wired, this ready.

Third quarter. Championship game. We're up by six, but the other team's breathing down our necks, and we need this drive.

Coach's voice barks in my headset, but I barely hear him. I already know the play. It's mine—the one I've run a hundred times in practice, the one I perfected. Fake handoff, roll left, keep it if the opening's there.

I lock eyes with my wide receiver, give him a barely-there nod, then snap the ball.

Time slows.

I fake the pass, tuck the ball against my chest, and bolt.

I see the hole. Wide open. Fifteen yards to the end zone, nothing but green turf and glory ahead. I push harder, legs pumping, lungs burning. This is it—the kind of moment quarterbacks dream about, the kind that gets you noticed, gets you recruited.

Then—

Pain.

A blinding, white-hot explosion in my knee, like someone's driven a crowbar straight into the joint. My body twists in the air, momentum yanking me sideways. The world flips, the sky where the ground should be, and then I slam into the turf, all breath ripped from my lungs.

I hear it before I feel it—the sickening pop. A dreadful sound you never want to hear from your own body.

Then the pain really kicks in.

Like fire, like knives, like the end of everything.

I can't move. My leg is twisted wrong, my hands digging into the grass, gripping at something, anything, to keep from screaming. The stadium noise fades, swallowed by the pounding in my ears.

I hear my name.

The announcer. The crowd. My teammates.

But all I can focus on is the agony, the cold realization sinking in my gut.

I don't even need the medics to tell me. I already know.

I know it the second the trainers rush the field, their faces tight with panic. I know it when Coach kneels beside me, his voice tight as he tries to keep me from completely losing it.

I know it when they load me onto the cart, and the whole damn stadium stands for me, clapping, cheering, chanting my name.

It doesn't feel like a victory.

It feels like a funeral.

Because Marcus Gray, future quarterback, star of Fairhope, the kid who was supposed to make it out—he died on that field.

And what was left of him?

Well, that guy had no idea where the hell to go next.

The road back to my rental cabin winds like it's trying to stall me, and maybe that's exactly what I need right now—time to think. I crack the window, letting the warm Fairhope air pour in, scented with pine and fried some-thing-or-other from Mabel's Diner down the block.

Annabelle. In a wheelchair. Laughing like the past didn't happen. Like we didn't happen.

And she didn't recognize me.

Not even a flicker.

It shouldn't sting as much as it does, but damn, it does. It's like someone took a scalpel and sliced clean through the part of me I thought had hardened over years ago.

I park under the crooked oak tree near the cabin and kill the engine. For a long time, I just sit there with my hands on the steering wheel, watching the shadows stretch over the grass. My plan was simple: stop by Fairhope, visit Mom's grave, say hi to Ethan, and bounce before the small-town nostalgia swallowed me whole.

But now? The plan's shot to hell.

I lean back and stare at the ceiling like it holds some kind of answer.

The city gave me everything I thought I wanted—a fancy apartment with too many windows, a job with a padded title and zero meaning, and nights filled with noise to drown out the quiet I never wanted to face. I tried to tell myself I was living. Thriving. That I didn't miss Fairhope or the people I left behind.

But the truth? My life there felt... hollow.

And now I know why.

It wasn't the city. It wasn't the career. It wasn't even the constant revolving door of dates and distractions.

It was her.

Annabelle Dawson.

The girl I left behind without so much as a real good-bye. The girl who made me believe in things like "forever" when I didn't even believe in myself. The one I kept buried under ambition and regret because remembering her felt like holding my breath for too long.

And now I've seen her.

And she's... not the same. But neither am I.

I think about what Ethan told me—how she'd been in that accident, how she lost her memory, how her dad practically locked her life in a cage of protection after I left.

I feel like the worst kind of coward.

I bailed when she needed me. I chased a dream and left her behind like she was part of a chapter I'd already closed. And maybe she doesn't remember me, but that doesn't change what I did.

I owe her more than a flash of guilt and a wave from across a coffee shop.

I owe both of us a second chance.

I grab my phone and cancel the return flight I booked for Friday.

Screw the plan.

I'm not leaving yet.

If there's even the slightest chance I can remind her of what we had—of who we were—then I'm staying. I'll find a way to be here, to prove that I'm not the same guy who walked away.

Fairhope was supposed to be a pit stop.

Now, it feels like it might be the starting line.

GHOSTS OF MEMORIES

Annabelle

I swear, Fairhope is like one giant group chat that never dies.

It doesn't matter how long someone's been gone—if they so much as step foot back in town, the whole place lights up like a Christmas tree with gossip. And today? That gossip is Marcus Gray.

I'm sitting outside The Cozy Bean, my go-to coffee shop, soaking in the late afternoon sun with a vanilla latte in hand. My friends are gathered around the table, chatting about the usual—who's dating who, Mrs. Thompson's latest conspiracy theory about the town council, how the new bakery is apparently overpriced but worth it—when Bree suddenly gasps like she's just uncovered the biggest scoop of the century.

"Did you guys hear? Marcus Gray is back in town."

My stomach suddenly has a bunch of butterflies fluttering about, and I have no idea why.

"Wait, Marcus Gray?" Lily raises an eyebrow, tossing a sugar packet into her coffee. "The quarterback?"

"The one and only," Bree confirms, leaning in like we're about to exchange top-secret information. "Ethan saw him outside the gas station yesterday."

I take a slow sip of my latte, trying to pin down why that name sounds so familiar. Marcus Gray. Marcus Gray. *I should know it, right?* It feels like I do. Like hearing a song from your childhood that you can't quite place, but it makes something stir deep in your gut.

"You mean the Marcus Gray who ditched this place without looking back?" Lily scoffs, stirring her drink. "Please. He probably rolled in just to flash his big city life at us and then disappear again."

I half-smile, but there's this weird tug in my chest, like an itch I can't reach. My mind tries to trace the name, find some memory to connect the dots—but it's just blank space.

"Annabelle, you okay?" Bree nudges me.

I blink, realizing I've been staring at the tiny crack in my coffee cup as if it holds the answer to the meaning of life. "Yeah, I'm fine. Just… I feel like I should remember him."

Bree shrugs. "Maybe you do. You did forget a lot after the accident." She says it casually, but I feel the way the words settle around me.

I forgot a lot.

Sometimes, I wonder how much.

I shake it off, forcing a grin. "Well, if he was that important, I probably wouldn't have forgotten him, right?"

They laugh, and the conversation shifts. But the feeling doesn't leave me.

It lingers.

Like a name on the tip of my tongue. Like a memory that almost wants to surface but stays just out of reach.

And for some reason, that unsettles me more than I'd like to admit.

Rehab days are the worst.

Not because I hate Samantha—she's great. She's patient and encouraging and doesn't make me feel like a complete lost cause. But some days, my body just doesn't cooperate, and it makes me want to throw something.

Today is one of those days.

"Okay, let's try again," Samantha says, kneeling beside me as I struggle to push myself up from the therapy bars. My arms burn, my legs barely budge, and my patience is officially on negative levels.

I grit my teeth. "Yeah, because the last five tries went so well."

"Attitude," she warns, but she's smiling. "Come on, one more time."

I blow out a frustrated breath and try again. My left leg trembles, my right leg stays completely useless, and I barely lift myself an inch before my muscles give up entirely.

Samantha steadies me before I can collapse back into the wheelchair. "That was better," she says, which is an obvious lie, but I appreciate it.

"Better than what? A statue?" I mutter, rubbing my palms over my thighs like I can will them to work properly.

She sighs. "Annabelle."

"I know, I know. Be patient. Progress takes time. Blah, blah, blah." I rest my head back, staring up at the ceiling tiles. "I just… feel like I should be more than this."

More than just a girl stuck in a wheelchair. More than someone who can't remember half of her life.

"Hey." Samantha nudges my knee, waiting until I look at her. "You are more. You always have been."

The words should help, but today, they don't. Because how do you know who you are when you can't remember who you were?

I don't know why I say it, but before I can stop myself, I blurt, "Do you know Marcus Gray?"

Samantha blinks at me. "Marcus Gray? The Marcus Gray? Of course. Star quarterback, Fairhope's golden boy." She tilts her head. "Why?"

I hesitate, gripping the arms of my chair. "I... don't know. Bree and Lily mentioned he's back in town, and I feel like I should remember him."

Samantha nods slowly. "Well, you two were close in high school."

I snap my head toward her so fast my neck almost cracks. "We were?"

She frowns. "You... don't remember that?"

"No!" I stare at her, a weird sort of panic creeping into my chest. "How close?"

She hesitates. "I mean... I don't know the details. But I remember seeing you two together a lot."

I grip my chair tighter. This feels wrong. Like something important is missing, something I should know.

I shake my head. "Why wouldn't my dad tell me that?"

Samantha's lips press together, like she wants to say something but doesn't.

That alone makes my stomach turn.

I feel like I'm standing at the edge of something big.

And I don't know if I'm ready to fall in.

Later that night, I'm restless.

It's one of those nights where my body is exhausted, but my mind? Wide freaking awake. That weird conversation with Samantha won't leave me alone.

Marcus Gray.

I know that name. I feel it. But every time I try to grasp

at something—a memory, a feeling, anything—it slips through my fingers like sand.

I sigh and roll my chair over to the bookshelf in my room. Most of my old stuff was cleaned out after the accident, but my dad had put together a scrapbook, hoping it would help me piece my life back together.

I pull it off the shelf and flip through it.

Birthdays. Dance recitals. Family vacations. The usual.

But then—tucked between a prom picture and some random notes from high school—I find something I don't remember seeing before.

An old, faded photograph, almost buried between the pages.

I tug it free and stare.

It's me. Standing near the lake, my feet in the water, smiling like I've never been happier. And next to me—some guy.

Tall. Strong. Familiar.

His arm is around me, and I'm leaning into him like it's the most natural thing in the world.

My heart pounds as I flip it over.

In messy, smudged ink, two names are written on the back: Annabelle & Marcus—In their summer glory.

I suck in a sharp breath.

Marcus.

The name that's been haunting me all day.

I trace my fingers over the faded ink, my skin tingling like my body knows something my mind refuses to remember.

Why can't I remember this?

Who was Marcus Gray to me?

And why does it feel like losing him was a bigger loss than I ever realized?

The photo sits in my lap like it weighs ten pounds. My fingers tremble around the frayed edge, like if I grip it too tight, it'll vanish—or worse, tell me something I'm not ready to hear.

Me and him. Laughing. Holding hands like it's the most natural thing in the world.

I trace the curve of my own smile in the photo. It's so *me* and somehow... not me at all. My hair's longer, my cheeks brighter, and my eyes—there's something in them I can't quite name. It's joy. It's safety. Maybe even love.

And Marcus?

That name alone—it scratches at something deep inside my brain, like a door trying to creak open but rusted shut. He doesn't look much like he did in the photo. His dark hair's the same, but his muscles are more toned, and those blue eyes... even though I saw him for the briefest moment the other day, I'm sure there were more emotions there, and more conviction... he grew up like the rest of us, I guess.

I squint harder at the image, willing it to unlock something. A laugh. A voice. The way he said my name. Anything.

And for the briefest second—*there*—a flicker.

I see myself in a truck. Passenger side. The radio's loud. My legs are in his lap, bare feet on the dash. He's driving one-handed, grinning, looking at me like I hung the moon. We're shouting lyrics to something... something stupid and happy.

Then—

Pain.

A sharp stab in my head, like someone just jammed an ice pick through my temple.

I gasp, clutching the side of my head as the image vanishes as quickly as it came.

No, no, no.

I squeeze my eyes shut, hoping it'll come back, but all that's left is a dull ache and my own uneven breath. It's frustrating, like a dream you forgot the second you opened your eyes.

Toby, curled up on the rug nearby, lifts his head and whines softly. Even he can tell something's off.

"I'm okay," I whisper, more to myself than him.

But I'm not. Not really.

Because that wasn't just a memory—it *felt* like something real. Something mine.

I look down at the photo again, and now it's almost speaking to me. Not literally, but with meaning. Weight. Like it's proof of something I've been missing, whether I remember it or not.

Marcus Gray.

He's not a stranger.

He *was* something. Someone.

And even if I can't remember what that means yet, I know one thing with the kind of certainty that lives in your bones:

This matters.

He matters.

CROSSING PATHS

MARCUS

*I*t's funny how life works sometimes.

If you'd asked me a few years ago where I thought I'd be at twenty-five, I'd have said something cocky, like "catching touchdown passes in front of fifty thousand screaming fans." Definitely not handing out towels and sports drinks at Fairhope's tiny, rundown sports center.

Yet here I am. Mr. Big Shot Marcus Gray, king of washed-up quarterbacks, stepping through the creaky doors of Fairhope Fitness like it's a dream come true.

The lobby hasn't changed much since high school. Same faded posters on the walls, same scratched-up hardwood floors, same smell of rubber mats and sweaty gym socks. But weirdly, there's something comforting about that familiarity—like the place never stopped waiting for me to come back, even when I swore I never would.

"Marcus!" Ethan's voice rings out, way too cheerful for 8:00 AM. "Welcome to your glamorous new job."

I turn to see him grinning behind the reception desk, spinning lazily in an old office chair. "You look like you're enjoying this way too much," I say, tossing my backpack onto a bench.

"Watching Marcus Gray humble himself? Hell, yeah. I might even take pictures."

"Funny," I mutter, leaning against the counter. "You know, when you said they needed help around here, I was thinking more like personal training. Less towel duty."

"Aw, come on. It's character building," Ethan jokes, leaning back with his hands behind his head. "Besides, it'll help you stay humble when those big-city dreams start knocking again."

I snort. "Right, thanks for the life lesson."

He nods toward the wall. "At least your picture's still up."

My gaze slides over to the faded photo hanging among other athletes who've come and gone—Fairhope's pride, frozen in time. I'm front and center, flashing a cocky grin I hardly recognize anymore. Beside me, teammates whose names I've forgotten smile like we'd stay young forever.

"That guy was an idiot," I say quietly, mostly to myself.

Ethan's chair creaks as he leans forward, his tone softening. "Nah, he just didn't know better yet."

"Yeah, well, he learned." I shrug, trying to brush off the heaviness settling on my shoulders. "Fast."

"Marcus, you're here now," Ethan says simply, slapping the desk as if that closes the discussion. "Might as well make the most of it."

I know he's right, but making the most of anything in Fairhope feels a lot like admitting defeat. Still, I owe it to myself—and maybe to her—to stick around and figure things out.

As if on cue, my eyes catch the therapy schedule tacked behind the desk, and my pulse speeds up.

Annabelle Dawson—10:30 AM Physical Therapy.

"You good?" Ethan asks, following my gaze.

"Yeah." I try to keep my voice steady, casual. "Just... didn't expect to run into Annabelle so soon."

Ethan gives me a knowing look. "You didn't exactly come back for the job, Marcus."

"No kidding," I mutter, pushing away from the counter before the conversation gets any deeper. "I better get started. Wouldn't want these towels to fold themselves."

Ethan chuckles, shaking his head as I walk down the hallway, leaving him behind. My heart's doing some kind of Olympic gymnastics routine in my chest as I step into the back office and pull on a faded Fairhope Fitness shirt— the official uniform of washed-up hometown heroes everywhere.

I've barely gotten settled into my mundane tasks when the bell above the door chimes. My stomach tightens, and I glance up automatically, like some pathetic high schooler hoping to see his crush walk through the door.

Only, that's exactly what happens.

Annabelle wheels herself into the lobby, chatting softly with Samantha, the therapist Ethan introduced me to yesterday. My throat tightens as I watch her from afar, noticing all the little things that haven't changed—the way her hair catches sunlight, the faint smile she gives everyone, even strangers.

Then again, I guess I'm a stranger now too.

Annabelle's gaze drifts toward me briefly. Her eyes narrow in mild confusion, like she's trying to place my face, and for half a second, I hold my breath, hoping for some flicker of recognition.

Nothing.

She looks away again, chatting comfortably with Samantha as they disappear down the hall toward the therapy room, leaving me standing there feeling ridiculous and invisible.

"Smooth, Gray," I mutter, shoving a pile of towels into the basket harder than necessary.

The sensible part of me knows this isn't her fault. It's mine. I'm the one who left town, walked away, didn't look back. But the selfish part of me—the part that's always loudest—still wishes she'd remembered something. Anything.

"Hey, you okay?" Ethan asks quietly, coming up behind me.

"Sure. Just realized how pathetic I look," I say dryly, forcing a grin I don't feel.

Ethan shrugs. "You can't rush these things, man. Especially not with Annabelle."

"I know." I sigh, leaning against the table. "Doesn't make it suck less."

Ethan claps me gently on the shoulder. "Well, good news is, you're sticking around. Plenty of time to make things right."

"Or screw things up worse," I counter.

He laughs softly. "That too."

He's right, of course. Ethan's always been the steady voice of reason. But reason isn't exactly my thing.

I glance toward the therapy room again, picturing Annabelle struggling through her exercises, frustrated but determined, completely unaware that I'm here, quietly rooting for her.

And as I fold yet another towel, I make myself a promise. Maybe I don't deserve another chance, but I'm here. And I won't run this time.

I'm going to find a way back into Annabelle's life. Even if it means starting from scratch, one folded towel at a time.

~

I spend the next hour doing my job—or pretending to, anyway—keeping busy folding towels, refilling water bottles, and resisting the urge to glance over at the therapy room every five seconds. But who am I kidding? I'm not exactly fooling anyone, especially not Ethan, who keeps shooting me looks like he thinks I'm seconds away from doing something reckless.

He might be right.

Eventually, I hear soft voices coming from the therapy area. My heart jumps, and before I can think better of it, I'm already walking toward the sound.

I hover in the doorway, arms crossed, trying to look casual when I'm anything but. Samantha's gently guiding Annabelle through exercises, her voice calm and patient. Annabelle's forehead is creased in frustration, her cheeks flushed as she grips the parallel bars, fighting with every ounce of strength to get her body to cooperate.

It guts me to watch her like this—so determined, yet clearly struggling. The Annabelle I remember was fearless, always dancing around, never sitting still for a minute. Seeing her confined like this twists something deep inside me.

"Hey," I finally say, stepping into the room like I'm not feeling a million things at once. "You two need anything?"

Samantha glances up, smiling warmly. "We're okay, Marcus. But thanks."

Annabelle's eyes flicker toward me, cautious, guarded. Her expression tightens slightly, confusion clouding her face again. I hate seeing it—that brief second where she tries so hard to place me, only to fail.

"You work here now?" she asks softly, curiosity creeping into her voice.

"Yeah," I say, shrugging. "Guess you could say I'm rediscovering my roots."

It's supposed to be funny, but it lands flat. Annabelle

nods awkwardly, eyes dropping to her lap as a silence stretches between us. Samantha catches my eye, clearly sensing the tension.

"You know, Marcus used to be pretty good at training," Samantha says brightly, obviously trying to lighten the mood. "Maybe he can offer some motivational tips."

Annabelle raises an eyebrow, a hint of a smile playing at her lips despite her obvious discomfort. "Motivational tips, huh?"

"Hey," I say, holding up my hands with mock serious-ness. "I was legendary for my pep talks back in high school."

She tilts her head, skeptical, but a spark of amusement flashes across her eyes. "Were you now?"

"Oh, definitely." I step closer, careful not to crowd her. "My strategy was pretty simple. Yell louder, run faster, and pretend you know what you're doing."

Annabelle actually laughs—quietly, hesitantly—but it's there. That soft, genuine sound loosens something in my chest. Samantha grins, giving me a subtle thumbs-up as she steps aside, pretending to adjust some equipment.

"I'll keep that in mind next time I'm getting frustrat-ed," Annabelle says softly, eyes meeting mine for just a second longer than before. There's a cautious curiosity there, something vulnerable hidden beneath her polite smile.

"You should," I reply gently. "Works every time."

She studies me again, more closely this time. I wonder if she's sensing something deeper, something beyond the casual friendliness I'm trying to project. But just as quickly, she seems to shake herself free of whatever thought she's having.

"Well," she says, glancing down at her chair, cheeks flushing slightly. "Thanks. For the tip, I mean."

"No problem," I say, feeling more awkward than I want to admit.

Samantha returns, interrupting before the silence can grow again. "Alright, Annabelle, let's wrap up for today."

Annabelle nods quietly, her gaze drifting toward the floor. "Yeah. Sounds good."

I step back to give her space as Samantha helps her back into the wheelchair. My gut twists again, watching the careful, practiced way Annabelle moves, how much effort she hides behind that brave face.

They pass by me, Samantha giving me an encouraging nod, but Annabelle stops suddenly, looking up. Her eyes are softer now, curious but hesitant. Something about her expression makes my pulse pick up speed.

"I, um..." Annabelle hesitates, clearly debating something internally. "Thanks again. I really did need a laugh."

"Anytime," I say softly, holding her gaze. "Seriously."

She nods slowly, offering a shy, uncertain smile as she rolls away. I stay there long after they disappear down the hallway, trying to catch my breath, replaying every word we exchanged.

It's a start, I think, a small, cautious first step. But it's something.

And for the first time since I came back to Fairhope, I feel a flicker of real hope.

I'm pretty sure there's a special place in hell for guys like me—guys who stand around gyms obsessively watching the girl who doesn't even remember them. But here I am anyway, leaning casually against the wall, pretending to reorganize water bottles for the hundredth time as Annabelle finishes packing her things.

She wheels toward the exit slowly, eyes scanning the

lobby like she's searching for something—or maybe some-one. My pulse jumps. I'm not about to miss this chance, so I quickly push off the wall and pretend I'm just casually walking in her direction.

"Heading out?" I ask, forcing my voice to sound casual. "Need help?"

She pauses, looking up at me with a guarded expression. "I'm okay, thanks."

"Of course," I say, taking a breath. "Hey, listen, I was just thinking..." I pause awkwardly, shoving my hands in my pockets, feeling like a fifteen-year-old again. "Would you maybe wanna grab coffee sometime?"

She hesitates. I can practically see the wheels turning in her head, weighing curiosity against caution. "Coffee?" she echoes softly, confusion coloring her voice. "Just us?"

"Yeah," I reply quickly. "Totally casual. No pressure or anything. It's just—" I break off, swallowing hard. "We clearly knew each other once. Maybe talking could help jog your memory?"

Annabelle studies me carefully, her eyes thoughtful. "You really want me to remember you that badly?"

The honesty catches me off guard. I laugh nervously, rubbing the back of my neck. "Is it that obvious?"

"Kind of." A faint smile tugs at her lips. "But...maybe you're right. It might help fill in some blanks."

Hope spikes in my chest. "Yeah?"

"Yeah." She nods slowly, looking slightly embarrassed. "Okay. Let's do coffee."

"Great," I say, trying—and failing—to keep the eager-ness out of my voice. "Tomorrow afternoon, maybe? At The Cozy Bean?"

"Sure," she says softly, her smile growing a little stronger. "That sounds good."

We stare at each other awkwardly for another second

before she clears her throat, clearly feeling the same nervous tension.

"See you tomorrow, Marcus," she says quietly, testing my name on her tongue, almost as if she's trying it out for the first time.

"Yeah," I say softly, holding her gaze. "See you tomorrow, Annabelle."

I watch her go, my heart hammering in my chest, part relief, part anxiety.

Coffee tomorrow.

It's just coffee. No big deal.

But as the door swings closed behind her, I realize just how big a deal it really is.

Because tomorrow might be the day Annabelle Dawson finally starts remembering me—or it could be the day I lose her all over again.

WHISPERED TRUTHS

Annabelle

I get to The Cozy Bean way too early, like the anxious mess I clearly am, and I spend the first five minutes obsessively rearranging sugar packets on our table. The barista, Jenna, keeps glancing over with this amused look, probably wondering why I'm acting like a teenager on a first date. But it's not a date. Just coffee. With a guy who apparently knew me once—only I don't remember him at all. Totally normal stuff.

I sigh, forcing myself to sit back and quit messing with the sugar. I don't even know why I said yes to this. Maybe it's curiosity, or maybe it's that weird tugging sensation in my chest every time I hear Marcus's name.

Or maybe I'm just going insane. That's possible too.

The door jingles open, snapping me out of my thoughts. Marcus walks in, casual and effortlessly confident, but with this nervous look in his eyes that I immediately like more than I should. He spots me and smiles—a crooked, charming smile—and the butterflies in my stomach flutter wildly.

"Hey," he says, approaching our table slowly, hands in his pockets like he's not sure what to do with them. "You got here early."

"Yeah, well, I figured one of us should," I joke, trying to break the weird tension.

He chuckles softly. "Fair enough. You still drink vanilla lattes, right?"

I blink at him, startled. "How did you—?"

He looks sheepish. "Lucky guess?"

"Uh-huh," I say, raising an eyebrow. "Sure."

He grins and goes to order our drinks. I watch him, trying to match this Marcus—the charming, slightly awkward guy—with the cocky quarterback everyone keeps telling me about. Nothing lines up, but I guess people change. I mean, I did. Even if I don't remember how.

He comes back with our coffees, sliding mine over. "Vanilla latte, extra foam."

"Thanks." I take a cautious sip, grateful for something to do with my hands.

He leans back, eyes warm but cautious. "So…this is weird, right?"

"Oh, thank God you said it," I breathe out, laughing softly. "Yeah. It's incredibly weird."

He relaxes a bit, clearly relieved. "Good. Glad we're both awkward about this."

"So, how exactly do we know each other?" I ask carefully. "I mean, I found that old picture, and Samantha said we hung out. But… that's all I've got."

His smile fades slightly, and I feel a pang of guilt. It must be hard for him, too—talking to someone who doesn't remember him. "We were friends," he starts. "Really good friends. Especially senior year. We used to hang out by the lake a lot."

He pauses, waiting for some kind of reaction. I nod slowly, encouraging him to go on, but I still feel disconnected. It's like hearing someone describe a movie you never watched.

"Once, we borrowed your dad's fishing poles and spent the whole afternoon trying to catch something—anything." Marcus laughs, shaking his head at the memory. "We were awful at it, ended up soaked, and you fell into the water and pulled me in too. Your dad was furious."

I smile faintly, trying to picture it. It's fuzzy, just shadows of laughter, water splashing, the warmth of sunshine. "It feels… familiar," I admit, embarrassed. "But I can't grab hold of anything."

His expression softens. "That's okay. I'm not expecting miracles. It's just nice talking about it again."

I stare into my coffee, my fingers tracing the rim of the cup nervously. "Did we… Were we just friends?"

Marcus's cheeks flush, and for a second, he looks unsure how to respond. "Uh, I mean…mostly."

"Mostly?" I raise an eyebrow, feeling my own cheeks burn a little. "What does that mean?"

He chuckles awkwardly, rubbing the back of his neck. "I don't know. It was complicated. Your dad wasn't exactly a big fan of mine, even back then."

"Yeah, he's protective," I admit. "Especially now."

Marcus nods, something cautious and vulnerable in his eyes. "I get it. I'm not exactly the guy any dad wants around their daughter."

I glance up, startled by the hurt I sense in his voice. Before I can ask what he means, he shifts the conversation quickly.

"Anyway, we don't need to unpack all that yet." He smiles. "How about something simpler? You remember those bonfires at Ethan's?"

I laugh, grateful for the lighter topic. "Yeah. Well, sort of. Mostly that Lily always burned the marshmallows and pretended she meant to."

Marcus laughs too, nodding enthusiastically. "Exactly. She always insisted charred marshmallows were gourmet."

We talk for a while, laughing over small-town memories that feel both real and imagined. It's easy talking with him. Too easy. It makes me nervous how comfortable he feels already.

But every once in a while, when our eyes meet, there's this flash of inexplicable recognition, like I know there's something there, but I can't quite point at it. There's something he's holding back, and something inside me wants desperately to reach out and grab it.

The conversation drifts to quieter topics, Marcus describing random moments from our summers—lazy afternoons, sunsets by the lake, drives around town blasting terrible music.

"Do you remember that one night we snuck out to watch that meteor shower?" he asks softly, eyes bright with nostalgia. "It was cold, middle of November, and you stole your dad's truck—"

Something flickers at the edges of my mind, and suddenly, I'm somewhere else. A flash, quick and vibrant. The crisp air. My heartbeat racing from the thrill of rebellion. The scratchy wool of a blanket wrapped around my shoulders.

"Annabelle?"

I blink, shaken from the memory—or whatever that was—back to Marcus's concerned gaze. "Sorry. I just…for a second, it felt familiar. Like déjà vu."

He leans forward, his expression hopeful but gentle. "Really?"

"Yeah." I press my hand against my forehead. "Just bits and pieces. I can't really put it together."

Marcus nods, careful not to push too hard. "Well, it's something, right?"

"Yeah, I guess," I murmur, feeling suddenly over-

27

whelmed. "It's just frustrating. Feeling like my life is one big puzzle, and I've lost all the important pieces."

He hesitates, then slowly reaches across the table, his fingertips lightly touching mine. The warmth of his hand sends an unexpected jolt through me. My breath catches.

"Hey." his eyes are serious but kind. "You'll find those pieces. One at a time."

I stare down at our fingers, unsure how to respond. Marcus's touch feels strangely comforting, almost familiar. Like a long-forgotten song that still manages to calm me.

But guilt flares up quickly, sharp and insistent. I pull my hand back gently, feeling embarrassed and conflicted. "Sorry," I whisper.

"No, don't be," Marcus says. "I get it."

"It's just—" I start, then hesitate. "My dad's been through so much with me, you know? He worries a lot. Especially about people he thinks might stir things up."

Marcus smiles faintly, understanding clear in his eyes. "People like me?"

"Exactly," I admit. "And I can't exactly blame him. I don't remember you, Marcus, but something tells me you were important to me. And that scares me. Because if I can't remember why, how am I supposed to trust myself?"

Marcus studies me, absorbing my confession with a patience that both surprises and comforts me. "You don't have to rush. Trust your gut. If it feels right, we keep talking. If it doesn't, I step back. It's your call."

I let out a shaky breath, grateful for the respect in his words. "Thanks. That helps."

Marcus smiles, leaning back again, easing the tension. "No problem. After all, you're still the bossy one around here."

I laugh, shaking my head. "Am I?"

"Absolutely," he insists, eyes sparkling with playful mischief. "You were always bossy, especially when we tried cooking at Ethan's. You'd stand there yelling at us to get the measurements right. We never listened, though."

Another spark of memory nudges my mind—the smell of burnt brownies, laughter echoing through Ethan's kitchen, Marcus's flour-covered face grinning sheepishly.

I smile, feeling calmer again. "Maybe I remember that too. A little."

Marcus grins. "Good. See? Progress."

And for the first time, sitting here with him feels less like a puzzle and more like an adventure. One I might just be brave enough to take.

At least, until the coffee shop door slams open loudly enough to make us both jump—and my father storms in, eyes blazing, jaw set like stone.

My stomach sinks instantly, and Marcus stiffens beside me.

Oh, this is not going to be good.

"Dad," I whisper, my cheeks burning as every single head in The Cozy Bean swivels toward us. Marcus straightens in his seat, clearly bracing himself. "What are you doing here?"

My father ignores my question completely, his narrowed eyes fixed entirely on Marcus. "What part of 'stay away from my daughter' didn't you understand, Marcus?"

Marcus calmly rises from his chair, his posture respectful but firm. "Sir, we were just talking. Annabelle deserves the truth about—"

"The truth?" Dad scoffs, voice low and dangerous. "You think you're helping her? She was doing fine before you came back. Now you're dragging her into things she doesn't need to remember."

I shrink back in my chair, humiliation washing over me. "Dad, please," I say quietly, desperate to diffuse the situation. "Marcus was just trying to help me remember some things."

He finally looks at me, anger flashing momentarily into hurt. "Annabelle, you don't understand what you're getting into. I kept this from you for your own good. He's not good for you. He never was."

The hurt in Marcus's eyes hits me hard. He doesn't argue back, just stands silently, accepting my dad's words like a punch. Guilt stabs through my chest. "Dad, we were just having coffee," I insist again, my voice shaking. "Nothing happened."

"Nothing happened yet," Dad corrects, sharply. "Annabelle, it always starts small. Coffee, a few conversations, next thing you know he's breaking your heart again and disappearing like last time."

I freeze. Marcus flinches visibly at the words. "What do you mean 'breaking my heart'?" I'm suddenly feeling dizzy. "You said Marcus was just a friend."

My father hesitates, clearly caught off guard. "It was complicated. It doesn't matter now."

Marcus breaks the tense silence. "Maybe it matters to her."

My father turns on Marcus again, voice icy. "You lost any say in what matters to my daughter the day you walked out of this town and left her behind."

Marcus's jaw tightens, but he doesn't fight back, just nods slowly. "I understand you're upset, Mr. Dawson, and I respect that. But Annabelle's an adult. She deserves to make her own decisions."

My father glares at him, his eyes cold. "Stay away from her, Marcus. I won't ask you again."

With that, Dad takes the handles of my wheelchair with a firmness that startles me, maneuvering me out of the coffee shop before I can protest any further. The sympathetic glances from the other customers burn my face as we leave. I don't even dare look back at Marcus—I'm too embarrassed, too confused, too hurt.

We're halfway to the car before Dad finally speaks again. "I'm sorry you had to see that, Annabelle. But trust me, Marcus Gray isn't someone you want in your life."

I stare down at my lap, biting back a thousand questions. But all I can manage is a quiet, defeated, "How would I even know, Dad? I can't remember."

He sighs deeply, sounding suddenly weary. "Maybe that's a blessing, sweetheart."

I don't say anything else, letting silence stretch between us, thick and suffocating, all the way home.

Back in my room, the silence feels deafening. I sit at my desk, staring blankly at the faded photograph from the scrapbook—Marcus and me, smiling, carefree, wrapped in each other's arms by the lake. I trace my fingers over his face, wishing desperately for answers.

What could have happened between us to make my father react so strongly?

I know Dad means well, but something about his anger feels off. Too strong, too personal. Marcus was kind, careful, respectful—nothing like the careless heartbreaker my father described. And the memories Marcus stirred felt warm and comforting, not painful.

My phone buzzes suddenly, making me jump. It's Marcus, texting cautiously:

Marcus: Are you okay? I'm sorry if I made things worse.

My heart aches. I tap out a reply quickly.

Not your fault. I'm sorry my dad acted that way.

His response comes fast, gentle and reassuring.

Don't apologize. I understand. Just wanted to make sure you're okay.

I stare at my screen, hesitant, then type another message.

Did you really break my heart?

The reply takes longer this time, and my stomach twists nervously as I wait. Finally, his message appears.

I made mistakes. I left town, and it hurt you. But there's a lot more to it than that. If you're willing, I'd like a chance to explain everything sometime.

I hesitate. Everything inside me screams to say yes, to get the whole truth. But my father's words still ring in my ears, heavy and insistent. Yet, deep down, a stubborn voice whispers that I deserve answers—not just my father's version but Marcus's too.

Before I can second-guess myself, I reply:

Yes. Soon.

His answer appears immediately:

Whenever you're ready.

I set my phone aside, feeling lighter and heavier all at once. Something big is waiting for me—truths that will either set me free or leave me more lost than before. But one thing is certain—I can't stay in this half-life forever, guarded by secrets and missing pieces.

I take a deep breath, preparing myself. Whatever Marcus reveals, I'm ready to hear it—even if it changes everything.

NEW BEGINNINGS

Marcus

I've never been good at handling rejection—
mostly because, until my knee blew out, I rarely
had to. But having Annabelle's dad publicly warn me off
in front of half the town was a special kind of humiliation.
Now, I'm pacing around Ethan's living room trying to
make sense of things and channel my anger, feeling both
pissed off and pathetically helpless.

"You're gonna wear out the floorboards if you keep
pacing like that," Ethan says, lounging casually on his ratty
couch, sipping from a soda. "Sit down before you give me
anxiety."

"Dude, your house is nothing but anxiety," I snap back,
finally sinking into the worn recliner across from him. "And
Annabelle's dad officially hates my guts."

Ethan shrugs, annoyingly unfazed. "He always kinda
did. You just didn't care back then."

"I care now," I mutter, scrubbing a hand over my face.
"Annabelle barely knows who I am, and her dad's out here
painting me as some villain who's gonna ruin her life."

"Well," Ethan says, dragging the word out dramatically, "you did break her heart once, Marcus."

I shoot him a sharp glare. "Seriously, not helpful, man."

He holds up his hands in mock surrender. "Just saying. Look, if you want her to trust you again, you've gotta show her who you are now, not who you were then. Her dad's always gonna see the guy who ditched town. But Annabelle? She's still figuring things out. You've gotta give her something real, something she can see with her own eyes."

I lean back, sighing heavily. Ethan has always been annoyingly good at being right. "Fine. So, what's your brilliant plan? I show up on her doorstep with flowers and an apology card?"

Ethan snorts. "Oh, please. Give the girl some credit. She's not gonna be won over with cheesy gestures."

"Then what?" I groan, frustrated. "I'm running out of ideas."

Ethan grins wickedly, sitting forward with newfound enthusiasm. "Community stuff. The charity events, the town festivals. You've been helping with that stuff since you came back—let Annabelle see the Marcus Gray who volunteers with little league teams and helps old people with their yards."

I raise an eyebrow skeptically. "And you think that'll make a difference?"

He shrugs again, casual confidence oozing off him. "It'll show her you're not just some guy her dad hates. Let her see the good side—the side we both know you've always had. Even when you pretended otherwise."

"Yeah, right," I mumble, unable to fully hide my embarrassment. "You make me sound like a boy scout."

"Hey, even bad boys can have a heart," Ethan teases, chucking an empty soda can at me.

I bat it away, rolling my eyes but unable to suppress a grin. "Fine, whatever. Let's say you're right. How do I even get her involved?"

Ethan smirks, leaning back smugly. "Easy. You ask. Worst case, she says no."

"Or her dad shows up with a shotgun," I mutter darkly.

"Risk it," Ethan says seriously. "She's worth the risk, isn't she?"

I hesitate for just a second before nodding. "Yeah, she is."

He grins again, satisfied. "Good. Now go figure out which community thing to drag her into first."

I stand up, grabbing my jacket off the back of the chair, feeling slightly less hopeless. "You're annoyingly good at pep talks, Carter."

"Yeah, it's a gift," Ethan says, mock-bowing from the couch. "You're welcome."

I roll my eyes again, but as I head out the door, I feel lighter. Ethan's right. If I want Annabelle back in my life, I've gotta give her more than faded memories and apologies.

I've gotta show her the person I am now—the guy who actually deserves a second chance.

Two days later, I'm at the sports center again, nerves knotted tightly in my chest. Annabelle's scheduled for therapy this afternoon, and if I'm gonna ask her to get involved in community events, now's the time.

I spot her right away, sitting quietly by the window after her session, staring out at nothing in particular. She looks lost in thought, her brows furrowed softly. I feel a strange sorrow seeing her that way—like she's searching desperately for something she can't quite reach. I want to help her, but I don't know if I can.

"Hey," I say softly as I approach, trying not to startle her.

She jumps anyway, turning quickly to face me. "Marcus," she says, a hesitant smile forming. "You startled me."

"Sorry," I chuckle nervously, rubbing the back of my neck. "Didn't mean to."

She shakes her head slightly, the corners of her lips curving up more genuinely now. "It's okay. Just got caught up in my thoughts."

I nod slowly, my heart hammering. "Listen, I wanted to ask you something. If you're not comfortable, just say no. No pressure."

Her eyebrows lift slightly, curiosity replacing her earlier apprehension. "Okay…"

I take a deep breath, feeling strangely vulnerable. "There's a town festival this weekend—just something small. I usually help out, volunteering with the kids' games, handing out popcorn, stuff like that. It's kinda cheesy, but fun. Anyway, I was wondering if you'd want to come with me? Maybe help out a bit too."

She hesitates, clearly torn. "I'm not sure, Marcus…"

I scramble to reassure her quickly. "No expectations, Annabelle. Seriously. Just figured you might enjoy getting out a little, maybe see a different side of things. No pressure if it's too much."

She studies me, eyes thoughtful. "It's not that. It's just —my dad—"

I nod, understanding immediately. "Right. Look, if it helps, Ethan's gonna be there too, and a bunch of others. Totally casual, public setting. It's just community stuff, nothing major."

She bites her lip, debating internally. My heart pounds as I wait, praying she'll say yes.

Finally, after what feels like forever, she meets my gaze again, determination flickering in her eyes. "You know what? Okay. I'll come."

Relief floods through me, powerful enough that I almost sag against the nearby bench. "Really?"

She laughs at my obvious surprise. "Yeah. It sounds nice. And besides," she adds, voice quieter, "maybe seeing what you do around here will help me understand why everyone seems so intent on keeping us apart."

"Maybe," I hold her gaze carefully. "I just wanna show you who I am now, not just who everyone says I used to be."

She nods slowly, a small smile lighting her eyes. "I'd like that."

My chest feels lighter than it has in days, warmth spreading through me. "Great. It's Saturday at noon in the park. I'll pick you up?"

She considers it for some time and then nods. "Yeah. That'd be good."

"Okay," I say, unable to hide my relief and excitement. "It's a date."

Her cheeks flush just a little at my words, and I quickly backtrack, feeling my own face heat up. "Not a date-date. Just, you know, an outing. With people. Community stuff."

Annabelle's eyes sparkle, amusement outweighing her earlier hesitation. "Right. Totally casual."

I chuckle awkwardly. "Exactly."

She wheels herself away slowly, smiling her beautiful smile back at me once before disappearing out the door. I stay there for a moment, feeling like I just ran a marathon. But there's a thrill in it too—a new possibility blooming in the mess I've made of things.

Maybe Ethan's right after all. Showing Annabelle who I am now might just be the only way forward.

And right now, that's a chance I'm more than willing to take.

❧

Later that night, I'm lying awake, staring at the almost bare ceiling of my rented cabin. I could've stayed with my family, but things aren't great there. Dad couldn't make peace with the fact that his son wouldn't be a star athlete— to him, I'm a failure for life. It doesn't matter what I do; I can't make him believe in me, and I've given up trying.

Yet, here I am in Fairhope. But that's for... for Annabelle. My mind suddenly teleports to better times, disregarding the hopelessness of the present.

We're at the old sugar mill, the one on the edge of town where the fence is half-fallen and the wildflowers grow through the cracks in the pavement. No one goes there except us.

She's barefoot, her shoes tossed in the grass, walking along the rusted metal rail like it's a tightrope. Her arms are out for balance, her sundress fluttering in the wind, and she's smiling—at me, always at me.

"I'm gonna fall," she calls over her shoulder, laughing.

"No, you won't," I say, standing just behind her, hands out like I'm ready to catch her.

She glances down, one eyebrow raised. "You think you can catch me, Marcus Gray?"

I smirk. "Always."

She hops down, landing a little clumsily, right into my arms. And I don't let go right away. Neither does she.

We sit there for hours, legs tangled, fingers grazing over scraped knees and whispered dreams. She talks about traveling, about opening a little art shop in a town no one's ever heard of. I tell her I'll play college ball, and she can hang her paintings in our living room, and we'll eat cereal for dinner and forget to buy curtains.

She laughs and tells me that sounds like heaven.

Yes, it was heaven compared to the hell everything nosedived into after the accident. Sure, my career disappeared from right in front of me, but what hurt the most was losing Annabelle. I know I'm to blame for all this, and it makes it twice as hard.

My mind spirals into negativity faster than I imagined, but I suddenly remember the high school Annabelle daring me to catch her. I was certain at the time that I could.

And I'm certain even now that I can. I can give it a try. I can make her mine again... whatever it takes. She deserves everything.

FESTIVAL OF HOPE

Annabelle

*T*his town really knows how to throw itself a party, that's all I can think of as I take in the scene, Fairhope in its festive glory. No place like this.

The annual Fairhope Fall Festival is one of those things I vaguely remembered but hadn't actually experienced since before my accident. Now, wheeling through the bustling park, I realize just how much I've missed this kind of joyful chaos.

Families crowd around brightly colored tents, kids chase each other waving sticks of cotton candy, and there's the constant smell of popcorn mixed with fried dough wafting through the air and teasing the foodie in me.

I glance up at Marcus walking beside me, a ridiculous smile plastered on his face as if he's somehow responsible for all the excitement around us.

"You look way too happy," I tease, fighting back a smile myself.

He shrugs, eyes sparkling. "Hey, small-town charm is my secret superpower. It's impossible not to love this stuff."

"Clearly," I reply, rolling my eyes, though secretly I'm already charmed by how naturally he seems to fit in here.

Marcus leads me towards the center of the festival, past booths selling hand-knit scarves, homemade jams, and cider donuts. Occasionally, someone stops him with a hearty slap on the shoulder, asking him about his job at the sports center or mentioning how glad they are he's back in town. He smiles, answering patiently each time, making every conversation seem effortless.

"You know everyone here?" I finally ask.

"Pretty much," Marcus admits sheepishly. "Small town, remember?"

"Yeah." I'm suddenly wondering how it must've felt for him to leave all this behind. "I guess that means everyone knows you, too."

Marcus shoots me a thoughtful glance. "Or at least they think they do."

I pause, noticing the hint of sadness beneath his casual tone. "What does that mean?"

He hesitates, then smiles gently. "Sometimes people don't let you grow beyond who you used to be. That's why I wanted you here today. To see the person I am now."

I study him for a second, surprised by his vulnerability. "Who you are now seems pretty good to me."

Marcus laughs, relief evident in his eyes. "Good. Because this whole festival thing was Ethan's idea, and if it fails miserably, I need someone to blame."

"Don't worry, I'll help you blame Ethan," I promise, laughing.

For the first time in a long while, I feel genuinely at ease—like I don't have to try so hard to hold myself together. Marcus has a way of making me forget the wheelchair, forget my father's warnings, forget how incomplete I usually feel.

It's dangerous how much I like that feeling.

Marcus glances down at me, mischief in his eyes. "Alright, Dawson. Ready for some festival fun?"

I grin despite myself. "As long as you don't make me throw a ring over milk bottles or anything."

"No promises," he says cheerfully, guiding us deeper into the festival's joyful chaos.

～

I quickly learn Marcus wasn't kidding about his involvement with the town's kids. He takes me to a brightly decorated booth where kids are lined up, waiting eagerly. It's a makeshift football toss game, and Marcus immediately dives in, kneeling beside a little boy who's holding the ball like it might explode at any moment.

"You got this, buddy," Marcus encourages gently, adjusting the boy's grip. "Hold it tight, just like that."

I watch silently, struck by the ease with which Marcus interacts with these kids. He's patient and kind, praising each throw—even the wild ones that miss the target completely. Soon enough, he's got them all laughing, cheering each other on, and genuinely enjoying themselves.

It's a version of Marcus that feels entirely new to me. The star quarterback I've heard about, the rebel my dad warns me away from—those versions don't match the guy kneeling in the grass, patiently showing a six-year-old how to throw a spiral.

"Hey, Annabelle!" Marcus calls, waving me over. "You wanna give it a shot?"

"Oh, I don't think so," I laugh nervously, shaking my head. "Sports aren't exactly my strength."

"Come on," Marcus insists, grinning mischievously. "You're braver than you think."

The little girl beside him nods emphatically, handing

me a ball with big, hopeful eyes. "Yeah, Miss Annabelle, you can do it!"

Well, I'm officially trapped.

"Fine," I say, rolling my chair closer. "But remember, you asked for this."

Marcus chuckles, carefully helping me position myself. His touch is gentle, respectful, careful not to push me out of my comfort zone. "Alright, quarterback Dawson. Let's see what you've got."

I toss the ball awkwardly—it goes wide, bouncing harmlessly into the grass. But the kids erupt in loud cheers anyway, Marcus joining them enthusiastically.

I laugh, feeling warmth rush to my cheeks. "Well, that was embarrassing."

"Not at all." Marcus leans close enough that only I can hear. "It was brave."

I glance up, heart stuttering a little at the earnestness in his eyes. "Thanks," I whisper.

"No problem," he replies warmly, squeezing my shoulder gently before turning back to help another eager kid.

My stomach flutters, a confusing, thrilling sensation. Watching Marcus here, in this moment, something inside me melts. It's no longer just curiosity or nostalgia pulling me toward him—it's something deeper, something real.

Later, Marcus and I wander away from the games, my mind swirling with unexpected feelings. We find a quieter corner near a food truck selling apple cider, and I take a grateful sip, gathering my thoughts.

"You okay?" Marcus asks, noticing my sudden quietness.

"Yeah. Just thinking," I say honestly, studying him. "You surprised me today."

"How so?"

"You're different than what I imagined," I admit, feeling oddly shy. "Different from what my dad says."

Marcus looks down, kicking lightly at the grass. "Your dad's not entirely wrong, Annabelle. I messed up when I left. Badly. He's right to be protective."

"I get that," I say softly. "But... it doesn't seem fair that I can't make my own decisions about who you are now. You seem like you've changed."

He looks up, a cautious smile forming. "I have. Leaving taught me a lot. Getting injured, having to start over—it humbled me, made me realize what matters."

"And what matters to you now?" I ask, my voice barely above a whisper.

Marcus hesitates, meeting my gaze seriously. "Being honest. Making amends. Helping people. And—" He pauses, voice gentler. "Maybe earning your trust again."

My heart goes soft all over again, like it wasn't doing that already, but my mind isn't fully okay with that. I want so badly to trust him, but there's a lifetime of caution drilled into me by my father, warnings echoing loudly in my head. Am I betraying my dad's protection by opening myself up to Marcus?

I try to imagine how he must have been all those years back. Star quarterback bad boy... but why did he choose me then, as a friend or... something else? I wasn't a show-stopper of any kind.

"I want to trust you, Marcus," I finally whisper. "But my dad's warnings—they're hard to ignore."

He nods gently, understanding clear in his eyes. "I get it, Annabelle. I won't push you. But I'm here, however you need me."

I sigh softly, grateful but torn. "I wish I could remember us. It would make this so much easier."

Marcus offers a small, sad smile. "It'll come back. When you're ready."

I glance across the festival, taking in the joyful crowd, families laughing, couples holding hands. My father's protective voice lingers, but Marcus's quiet sincerity speaks louder. I'm caught between my loyalty to my dad and the genuine pull I feel toward Marcus.

Maybe it's time to trust myself more.

~

As the sun starts to set, Marcus leads me toward the old carousel near the park's edge. It's an antique, brightly painted, with horses frozen in cheerful mid-gallop. Nostalgia tugs at my chest as we approach, and Marcus notices immediately.

"You okay?"

"Yeah. It's just… familiar, somehow."

Marcus flashes a grin, helping me up onto a bench seat on the ride. "You loved this thing. Said it felt like flying."

"I did?" I ask, gripping the metal bar as the carousel begins to slowly turn.

"Yeah," Marcus murmurs, eyes distant as if seeing me in some faraway memory. "You always rode the blue horse. Named him Blueberry."

A sharp burst of recognition flashes through me, sudden and overwhelming. My heart races as images flood my mind—Marcus laughing beside me, holding my hand tightly as the carousel spun faster, wind tangling our hair, joy sparkling in his eyes. I feel his warmth, the safety of his touch, the thrill of happiness.

"Annabelle?"

I gasp, shaking myself free from the memory. "I— remember something."

Marcus's eyes widen, cautious hope flickering. "Really? What?"

"Us," I whisper, voice trembling. "Here, on this carousel. We were laughing. You held my hand."

He stares at me, eyes soft and serious. "Yeah. I did."

I press my hands against my temples, overwhelmed by the vividness of the memory. It's real, clear—Marcus and me, happy and free, before everything went dark.

"What else do you remember?"

Before I can answer, another flash hits harder—bright headlights, the sound of shattering glass, the sharp, sudden pain, darkness swallowing me whole. I gasp sharply, clutching the metal bar tighter.

"Annabelle!" Marcus's voice sounds distant, panicked. "What's wrong?"

"I—I don't know," I whisper shakily, eyes filling with tears. "I think I remember the accident."

A FLICKER OF THE PAST

Marcus

I've seen plenty of people look scared in my life. Hell, I've been scared myself more times than I'd ever admit. But nothing has ever hit me harder than seeing Annabelle gripping the carousel's metal bar like it's the only thing keeping her from breaking apart.

"Annabelle," I say again softly, stepping close enough that she can hear me over the cheerful music still spinning above our heads. Her face has gone pale, her eyes wide with fear and confusion. "Hey, hey, it's okay. I'm right here."

She blinks rapidly, eyes darting around as though she's just woken up from a nightmare. "Marcus, I—I saw it," she whispers, her voice trembling. "The accident. Just flashes. Lights. Glass breaking."

My body reacts to the pain she must have been experiencing, making me wince a little, but I quickly offer her my hand, gentle but firm. "Come on. Let's get you somewhere quiet."

She nods shakily, allowing me to help her off the

carousel and into her chair. Her breathing is still uneven, and guilt twists in my chest. Maybe coming here was a mistake. Maybe pushing these memories isn't fair to her.

We find a quiet spot away from the festival chaos, beneath the shade of a large maple tree whose leaves have already turned fiery shades of red and gold. The music and laughter feel distant here, and Annabelle seems to breathe a little easier.

"Better?" I ask, kneeling down in front of her.

She nods, exhaling deeply. "Yeah, sorry. That was just… intense."

"You don't need to apologize," I reassure. "Can you tell me exactly what you saw? Take your time."

Annabelle looks down at her hands, picking nervously at her sweater sleeves. "It was dark, rainy. I saw headlights, bright and sudden, and then I heard glass breaking. Everything went black." She pauses, closing her eyes tightly. "But before that, there was us—laughing on the carousel. You were holding my hand. I felt safe."

I swallow hard, touched deeply by her words. "That night, the night of your accident, I wasn't there," I admit quietly, feeling shameful again about the way I left. "But the carousel memory—yeah, that was real. We spent a lot of evenings here, Annabelle."

She glances up, studying me carefully. "Were we more than friends, Marcus? Please, just tell me."

I hesitate, torn between honesty and the fear of overwhelming her. But she deserves the truth. "Yeah," I admit. "We were. You were the only person who ever really saw through me—the only one who made me want to be more than just some cocky athlete."

She takes a shaky breath, her eyes full of questions. "Why didn't anyone tell me?"

"Your dad didn't want you to remember how badly I

hurt you when I left," I admit bitterly. "And I guess everyone else just respected his decision."

Annabelle sighs, frustration flickering in her eyes. "That's not fair."

"Life rarely is," I reply, sounding like a philosopher, unable to mask the sadness in my voice. "But I'm here now. I'm not going anywhere this time."

She studies me, kind of like a scientist assessing a specimen but with affection—cautious hope battling against old doubts. "Marcus, what else don't I know?"

A million answers crowd my mind, but instead of bombarding her with the messiness of the past, I take her hand gently, meeting her eyes with steady reassurance. "Plenty. But we'll figure it out together—slowly. One memory at a time, okay?"

She squeezes my fingers, seeming grateful for the promise. "Okay."

I spend the rest of the festival sticking close to Annabelle, careful not to overwhelm her but unwilling to leave her side. She slowly starts smiling again, relaxing bit by bit until some of the earlier panic fades from her face.

The sun dips lower, making our surroundings sparkle in the golden glow as we make our way slowly toward the exit. Annabelle seems quieter now, more reflective than shaken, but my nerves are still shot from seeing her so vulnerable.

"Thanks for today," she says, startling me a little. "Even with…everything. It was really nice."

"You're welcome." I smile. I'm just relieved she doesn't seem upset anymore. "Sorry, things got a little intense there."

Annabelle shrugs slightly, her smile sad but genuine. "I

think that was bound to happen eventually. It's not your fault, Marcus."

I stop walking and kneel beside her, meeting her eyes seriously. "Hey, whatever happens, I'm here. If you want to keep trying to remember, great. If it's too much, we back off. Your call."

She looks more thoughtful now, and a smile tugs at the corner of her lips. "Marcus Gray, when did you become such a good guy?"

"Hey, careful," I tease. "You might ruin my bad-boy reputation."

She laughs softly, eyes brightening. "You're definitely not helping your cause, you know."

I grin back at her, relief flooding through me. "Well, maybe I'm okay with that."

Annabelle tilts her head, considering something, almost hyper-focused. "You know, you never told me why you actually came back to Fairhope."

I take a breath, feeling vulnerable again. "Honestly? I didn't really have a plan. My knee injury was the end of football, and suddenly, I had no idea who I was without it. So I came back here, thinking maybe I could find some answers."

"And have you?" she asks softly.

I squeeze her hand lightly, smiling sincerely. "I'm getting closer."

Annabelle glances away, clearly battling with herself internally. When she finally speaks again, her voice is hesitant. "Marcus, can I ask you something personal?"

"Anything," I answer immediately, meaning it.

She hesitates a second longer, then meets my eyes firmly. "When you left town, did you ever think about me?"

The vulnerability in her question hits me squarely in the chest. "Every damn day," I say truthfully, voice rough.

"Leaving you was the hardest thing I ever did, Annabelle. Not a single day went by that I didn't regret it."

Her eyes widen slightly, absorbing my honesty. "Then why did you leave?"

"I was scared," I admit quietly, embarrassed but determined to be honest. "Scared I wasn't good enough for you. Scared you'd realize I was just some idiot jock with no real future. So I ran."

She sighs deeply, eyes gentle. "You were always more than that."

I swallow hard, touched beyond words. "Maybe. But it took losing everything for me to realize it."

Annabelle nods slowly, processing my confession with quiet acceptance. Finally, she smiles warmly, nudging my shoulder gently. "Well, better late than never, right?"

"Definitely," I whisper, grateful beyond words that she's giving me another chance.

We linger near the festival entrance, neither of us quite ready to say goodbye. Annabelle's expression is thoughtful, as if she's carefully weighing something important.

"You okay?" I ask, curious.

"Yeah. Just thinking," she admits. "Marcus, do you really think my memories will come back?"

I nod. "Yeah, I really do. It'll just take time."

She bites her lip, hesitating a moment. "What if we helped them along? I mean… deliberately."

I raise an eyebrow, intrigued but cautious. "What did you have in mind?"

Annabelle takes a deep breath, gathering her courage. "I think we should visit some of our old places—spots where we spent time together. Maybe being there will help trigger more memories."

Surprise and worry collide inside me, making my stomach flip. "Are you sure you're ready for that?"

She nods determinedly. "Yes. I need answers, Marcus. My dad's been keeping too much hidden from me, and I can't just sit around waiting anymore. I need to face it."

My heart races, both excited and terrified by her courage. "Okay. We'll take it slow, though, alright? No pressure."

She smiles, grateful. "Deal." I try to fist bump her like we used to back in the day.

Annabelle laughs at that—this short, sharp little giggle she tries to stifle with her palm—and for a split second, it happens. That time-travel effect. The kind that yanks you out of the present and drops you square in the middle of something you thought you'd forgotten but never really left.

And suddenly, I'm sixteen again.

We're lying side by side in the back of my beat-up pickup, parked behind the old drive-in that's been closed since 2003. The stars are out—like, really out—and she's tucked under my arm, wearing one of my old jerseys that swallows her whole.

"You ever wonder if the stars are watching us?" she asks, her voice dreamy, her finger tracing lazy circles on my chest.

I grin. "Only when I'm with you."

She snorts. "That was so cheesy."

"I'm serious!" I protest, laughing. "You bring out the poet in me."

She turns onto her side, propping her head up on her hand. "Okay, Shakespeare. Hit me with your best line."

"Oh, you want the good stuff?" I say, raising an eyebrow.

"Lay it on me."

I clear my throat dramatically. "Your eyes outshine every street-light in Fairhope. Your smile could end wars. Your laugh—" I pause for effect, "—could resurrect my will to do homework."

She loses it. Like full-on laugh-snorting.

I grin because that was the whole point. "You're welcome."

She rolls her eyes and leans in closer. "Alright, my turn."

I nod. "Impress me."

She puts a finger to my lips, fake-serious. "Your jawline could cut glass. Your hair belongs in a commercial. And your smirk—God help me—makes me forget basic math."

I throw my head back laughing. "I knew you were only dating me for my hair."

"And your truck," she adds with a wink.

"Ah, of course. A woman of class."

She curls into me again, quieter this time. "But seriously, Marcus... I think I'm falling for you."

My heart skips like three beats in a row. I don't even pretend to be cool about it.

I kiss the top of her head and whisper, "Too late. I already fell."

Snapping back to the present, I stand up, offering her my hand again. "Want to go check out a special place?" By that, I obviously mean the old drive-in. When old memories hit you in the feels, it's time to create new memories.

Annabelle looks a little confused and hesitates briefly, but then a small smile crosses her lips. "Why is it special?"

I squeeze her hand gently, heart pounding at the memory of our time there—carefree days, stolen kisses under the stars, sharing little secrets that hardly mattered. "You'll see."

I roll her toward my truck, and the spark never leaves her eyes. She doesn't remember our time together, but the feeling? The closeness? It's there in her heart, I'm sure about that.

That's enough for me, but I'll help her remember, join the pieces together. And make it better because I'm not running away this time.

REVISITING MOMENTS

Annabelle

*I*t's funny how a place you've completely forgotten can feel so familiar. When Marcus pulls his truck up to the old sugar mill on the edge of town, I think I've found my way into a movie I've watched a hundred times over.

My heart thumps hard in my chest as he helps me out of the truck, the wheels of my chair crunching softly over gravel and leaves.

"I remember this." I'm surprised by my own certainty. "We used to come here a lot, didn't we?"

Marcus smiles in his typical soft but sure fashion. "Almost every weekend. It was our spot, away from everything."

Looking around now, I understand why. The sugar mill is ancient, half-collapsed walls overgrown with ivy, rusted machinery scattered around like forgotten toys. It's peaceful here, hidden from Fairhope's prying eyes. The perfect secret hideaway for two teenagers trying to escape the world.

The other night, when we went to the old drive-in, I wasn't shocked to think it was a place we used to go to often when we were teens. I don't remember much, of course, but it felt familiar somehow... and now, looking around the sugar mill, I feel the same sense of familiarity.

Marcus carefully pushes me toward the old loading dock, stopping at the edge, looking out over the open field behind the mill. Golden sunlight spills across the tall grass, and I swear I can almost hear echoes of our laughter drifting through the air.

"You okay?" Marcus asks, noticing my thoughtful silence.

I nod as my throat tightens with emotion. "Just trying to put all the pieces together. It's like seeing parts of a puzzle scattered everywhere, but not knowing how they fit."

Marcus sits down beside me, stretching out his legs. "We used to sit right here for hours. You'd draw, and I'd complain about practice and how much pressure I felt."

"You complaining? Shocking," I tease, smiling at him.

He chuckles. "Yeah, I know. Hard to believe."

He grows quiet, eyes focused somewhere far away. "You always knew how to calm me down, Annabelle. Just being around you—everything felt clearer, lighter."

My cheeks heat slightly, heart fluttering at his words. "Did we ever talk about our futures? Like, dreams and stuff?"

Marcus glances at me, surprise flickering across his face. "All the time. You were gonna study art, maybe even go to Europe. I was gonna make it big playing football, get rich, famous... typical Marcus Gray dreams." He laughs bitterly, shaking his head. "Seems pretty silly now."

"It's not silly," I insist, nudging his arm. "We were just kids. Dreams change. People change."

"Yeah," he murmurs, meeting my gaze. "But some-times I wish they hadn't."

The sincerity in his eyes sends a shiver through me. And then, to make my mind feel more disoriented, my eyes land on a poster, something bluish, and it triggers vague memories.

Something... flickers.

A flash of blue and white. A large "Go Gray!" in thick, bold letters. Glitter—so much glitter. And my hands? Covered in it.

I blink, and it's gone—but something stays.

My heart thumps faster.

Another fragment. I'm sitting cross-legged on a bedroom floor, probably mine, surrounded by markers and poster boards. There's music playing. Loud. Fun. The kind of music you only put on when you're too in love to care about what's cool.

A voice—his voice?—laughs and says, "You spelled quarterback wrong again."

I throw a marker cap at him.

I think I'm wearing a jersey. His? It smells like him.

Then it cuts—hard.

Another blink, and I'm in the middle of a field. Bleachers. People yelling. I'm holding a rolled-up poster in one hand and clutching some-thing to my chest. My phone? A camera?

He runs past. Number 7. That smirk. That smile. His eyes find mine through the crowd.

And then, like every other time recently, it's gone again. Like it slipped between the cracks in the floorboards of my mind.

Marcus is looking at me with concern etched on his face. I turn away quickly, feeling overwhelmed. "Show me more." I gesture toward the mill.

Marcus helps me around the mill's perimeter, pointing out familiar spots—the wooden bench where we carved our initials, a rusted wheel where we used to sit, daring each other to tell secrets. Each memory tugs at something inside me, hints of recognition fluttering just out of reach.

Finally, he stops near a huge old oak tree at the back of the property. Its gnarled branches twist up into the sky, offering shelter beneath. Something about this tree grips my heart, fills my entire being with bittersweet longing.

"We spent our last afternoon here," Marcus says. "Before graduation, before everything changed."

I reach out, brushing my fingertips against the rough bark. Images flood my mind—a soft picnic blanket, sketchbooks scattered, Marcus laughing, carefree and young. I can almost feel his head resting on my lap, see the sunlight filtering through leaves above.

"It was perfect, wasn't it? It had to be," I whisper, throat thick with emotion. "You... you told me something about... about not forgetting me. Did you?"

Marcus's breath catches, eyes wide. "Annabelle, you remember?"

"Bits and pieces," I admit, voice shaking. "But it's coming back."

Marcus swallows hard, stepping closer. "That afternoon meant everything to me. It's why leaving was the hardest decision I ever made."

"Then why did you?" I whisper.

He looks away. "Because I thought you deserved better. Someone who wouldn't hold you back."

"That wasn't your choice to make." I'm firm, surprising myself with my intensity. "It was mine."

"I know that now," he says, regret clear in his voice. "But back then, I was just scared."

I reach out, taking his hand gently, our fingers tangling together naturally. "We both deserved better."

Marcus squeezes my hand, eyes gentle. "Maybe now we can have it."

The hope in his voice sparks something deep within me, making me want to believe in second chances.

～

We sit quietly beneath the old oak, the warmth of Marcus's hand comforting and familiar, although I can't say I remember his touch... only vaguely, maybe. But it eases me, makes me feel the warm fuzzies.

Neither of us wants to move, trapped in this delicate moment of fragile peace. This is a strange feeling, but this attraction toward him... it doesn't feel strange.

"You know," Marcus finally breaks the silence softly, eyes distant. "When I came back to Fairhope, I convinced myself it was just temporary. That I'd get closure and move on."

"But now?" I ask, heart hammering.

He looks down at our intertwined hands, smiling faintly. "Now I don't know if I ever really wanted closure. Maybe I just wanted you."

My breath catches, words stuck somewhere in my chest. Marcus meets my gaze, his eyes full of quiet longing. "Annabelle, I—" he pauses suddenly, swallowing whatever he was about to say. "Never mind. It's too soon."

Frustration builds a new fortress inside me, and this time, it might be harder to knock it down. "Marcus, please. I can handle honesty."

"I know, but I don't wanna rush this. You deserve to get your memories back without extra pressure from me."

"Okay," I say slowly, respecting his caution, even if it leaves me aching with curiosity. "But one day, soon, we're gonna have to talk about this."

Marcus squeezes my hand. "Promise."

We fall quiet again, watching sunlight dance across the grass. Despite the unanswered questions between us, sitting here feels right, as if our souls recognize each other in ways my memory can't fully grasp yet.

Eventually, Marcus helps me back into his truck, our silence comfortable now, each lost in thought. When we arrive home, he walks me to the door, pausing on the porch.

"Thanks for today," I say softly, glancing up at him. "It meant a lot."

"Anytime," Marcus replies gently, hesitating as if he wants to say more. Instead, he just smiles warmly. "See you soon?"

"Definitely," I promise.

He leaves, and I watch until his truck disappears down the road, heart full of conflicting emotions—hope, fear, confusion, longing.

That evening, restless and buzzing with unanswered questions, I find myself digging through the boxes of old keepsakes my dad stored away after the accident. I'd never really explored them before, too afraid of the unknown, but tonight feels different. Necessary.

I sift through photos, school assignments, drawings, and random souvenirs—each a small glimpse into a past that feels both mine and entirely foreign. Then, tucked beneath an old yearbook, my fingers brush against a worn envelope. I pull it out carefully, heart leaping as I recognize my own handwriting scrawled across the front:

Marcus

My pulse quickens as I carefully open it, unfolding the letter inside with shaking hands.

Marcus,

I'm not sure if I'll ever have the courage to send you this, but I need to write it anyway. You mean more to me than anyone else ever has. You see me—really see me—in ways I never thought possible. You make me brave. You make me hope.

No matter where life takes us, please remember that. Remember us. Because I can't imagine my life without you.

Yours always,

Annabelle

My breath catches painfully, tears stinging my eyes. I wrote this. I felt this. And somehow, it vanished from my mind completely.

Clutching the letter to my chest, I sit in stunned silence. Whatever Marcus and I had before my accident wasn't just friendship or casual feelings. It was real, deep, powerful. My heart recognized that today, even if my mind didn't fully remember yet.

I glance toward my phone, heart beating faster than a Formula One driver. I should call him, tell him what I found. But something holds me back. I need more answers first—answers my father has kept hidden from me for far too long.

With new resolve, I fold the letter carefully, slipping it into my bedside drawer. Whatever happens next, I'm ready. No more hiding from my past.

No more hiding from Marcus.

UNEARTHED LETTERS

Marcus

*W*hen Annabelle texted me that she'd found something important, I'd dropped everything and raced to her place. My heart's been thundering ever since I pulled into her driveway. I have no idea what to expect, but the way she sounded—anxious, vulnerable —makes me feel vulnerable as well.

She's waiting on the porch, clutching a small envelope tightly in her hand. She looks nervous, pacing awkwardly in her chair as I approach.

"Hey." I sit down on the porch step beside her and hold her hand. "What's going on?"

Annabelle hesitates, eyes wide and uncertain. "I found something—a letter. I wrote it. It's to you."

My stomach knots instantly. "To me?"

She nods, carefully unfolding the paper. "It was hidden in my old things. I don't even remember writing it, but…it feels real."

She hands it to me carefully, her fingers brushing mine. I unfold the worn paper slowly, my heart jumping at the familiar scrawl of her handwriting. As I read her words, a wave of memories crashes over me—stolen afternoons by the lake, casual conversations beneath the sugar mill's oak tree, promises made and broken.

I glance up at Annabelle, who watches me nervously. Her cheeks flush slightly, her eyes darting away, embarrassed.

"Annabelle, I—" My voice catches, emotion clogging my throat. "I never knew about this."

She meets my gaze again, biting her lip. "Do you remember anything from back then? Did you know how I felt?"

I exhale, trying to steady myself. "I knew you cared. But I didn't realize how much. Or maybe I did, and I was just too scared to face it."

"Why scared?"

"Because you were the only person who ever really believed in me," I admit, feeling raw. "And I didn't think I deserved it. You saw through the act, the cocky athlete persona. You believed in the guy underneath, even when I didn't."

The memories haven't faded for me. I remember how I was back then, and how it felt to be appreciated by someone like Annabelle. No one else cared—not even my father—at least, not for the real me. I don't know if I even did.

Ten Years back

It's late. I'm seventeen, still high off another Friday night win. We crushed the other team. I threw three touchdowns and ran one in myself. Everyone's losing their minds—parents, teammates, the damn school principal. My dad's standing near the edge of the field, arms crossed, jaw tight like usual. Not smiling. Not clapping.

He waits until everyone else is gone before walking over.

"That scramble in the second quarter," he says without preamble. "You almost fumbled."

My helmet's still in my hands. My sweat's not even dry yet. "But I didn't."

"You got lucky," he says. "Next time, keep your eyes on the left edge. Don't get sloppy."

That's it.

No "Good job." No "Proud of you." Just a reminder that whatever I do, it's still not enough.

I nod like I always do and head for the truck. The silence is thicker than the mud on my cleats.

Later, I'm sitting in my room, the sound of the crowd still ringing in my ears, but none of it meaning anything. I've got the trophy on my nightstand, the game ball in my duffel, and this awful knot in my chest like I just lost instead of won.

That's when she knocks.

Annabelle, with her too-big hoodie and that soft smile that somehow cuts through the noise.

"Thought you might need this," she says, holding out a burger from Dean's and a milkshake that's already sweating through the cup.

"Celebratory dinner?" I ask, raising an eyebrow.

She shrugs, stepping inside like she's done it a hundred times before. "More like emotional support calories."

She sits cross-legged on the floor, pulling a poster tube out of her backpack. "Also, I made you something."

I unroll it—bright blue letters, glitter everywhere (of course), and a cartoon version of me holding a football like a trophy.

It's ridiculous.

And it's perfect.

"You're not gonna tell me how I almost fumbled?" I ask, only half-joking.

She tilts her head, brows pinching. "Why would I do that?"

"My dad did."

She's quiet for a second. Then: "You didn't fumble."

"I could've."

"But you didn't."

I look at her, really look. She's not impressed by the stats or the

*hype or the badge of Fairhope's golden boy. She just sees me. The
tired, over-pushed, unsure kid under all the bravado.*

*And for the first time that night, I actually feel like I won
something.*

~

Present Day

Annabelle's eyes soften. "You really thought you
weren't good enough?"

I nod slowly, embarrassed but determined to be honest.
"Back then, yeah. I had big dreams but zero confidence
outside of football. You were the only person who saw past
all that. Losing you—that was my biggest regret."

She places her hand on my shoulder. "Marcus, this
feels so complicated. My heart recognizes you, but my
mind is still trying to catch up. How am I supposed to trust
myself, or you, when everything's so unclear?"

I take her hand in mine, desperate to offer reassurance.
"Trust yourself first. Take your time. I'll be here."

She smiles, grateful but still cautious. "Can I ask you
something else?"

"Anything."

"Did you ever feel the same way?" Her question is
nervous, uncertain. "About me?"

I pause, heart racing, knowing I owe her honesty now
more than ever. "Yeah. I did. More than I ever admitted to
myself. Leaving Fairhope meant leaving you, and it almost
destroyed me. I just didn't know how to stay."

She breathes out slowly, absorbing my confession. "And
now?"

"Now...I still feel it. Maybe even stronger. But you
deserve time. You need space to figure things out."

Annabelle looks down at our joined hands, thoughtful.

"You keep saying that. But Marcus, every time I'm with you, things become clearer—not more confusing."

I swallow hard. "Then we keep going, one step at a time."

"Okay." She smiles, looking more perfect than perfection itself, and my heart warms at the fact that the smile has a lot of hope in it.

~

The quiet between us isn't heavy anymore. It's soft. Familiar.

We sit shoulder to shoulder on the porch steps, watching the last of the sunlight fade behind Fairhope's sleepy streets. The air smells like jasmine and fresh-cut grass, and the distant sound of cicadas hums like background music.

Annabelle's fingers brush against mine—just barely— and I know she's still thinking. Still working through the things she hasn't said yet.

"You know," she says finally, her voice low, "my dad keeps saying you're dangerous. That you're someone I should've let go of a long time ago."

I glance sideways, not surprised. Just sad.

"And I get it," she adds, her eyes on the horizon. "He's scared. I was in that accident. I forgot everything. And now I'm sitting here with the guy who broke my heart once already."

I let out a slow breath, the truth sitting heavy on my chest. "I don't blame him. I'd probably hate me too."

She looks at me, brow creased. "You don't hate you. Why should he?"

"I left," I say. "You needed me, and I ran. That kind of thing doesn't disappear just because I came back."

She nods, slow and thoughtful. "Maybe not. But people change. You did."

I meet her eyes. "So did you."

Annabelle leans back on her hands, letting her shoulders relax a little. "I just wish he'd trust me enough to see that. To know I'm not seventeen anymore. I can decide what's good for me."

"You'll get there," I say. "It'll take time, but he loves you. He's scared of losing you again."

"I know," she whispers. "But sometimes I wonder— what if he's wrong? What if clinging to safety means I miss something good?"

I nudge her gently, smiling just a little. "Then we prove him wrong. We keep showing up. Together."

She chuckles, leaning her shoulder into mine. "Brave words for someone who still flinches every time my dad walks in the room."

"I *like* my spine intact," I say, deadpan. "But I'd still risk it."

That gets a real laugh, and I let myself soak it in for a second. I've missed this sound—the way her laugh fills a space like sunlight.

But then she grows quiet again, gaze drifting down to her hands.

"What if I never get it all back?" she asks softly. "The memories. The version of me who wrote that letter, who loved you with her whole heart and wasn't scared of anything?"

I shift closer, not letting go of her hand. "You don't have to be her again. I'm not the same guy you wrote to."

She glances up at me, eyes searching.

"I mean it," I say gently. "We can build something new. Something better. The Annabelle who's here now—the one figuring things out, who's brave enough to question everything? I'm already crazy about her."

Her cheeks flush a little, the kind of blush you don't try to hide. "You make it sound easy."

"It's not," I say honestly. "But it doesn't have to be easy to be worth it."

She's quiet a moment, but her shoulders relax. The tension in her jaw fades.

"You've really changed, Marcus," she murmurs. "You're... softer. Calmer. But still you."

"Blame Fairhope," I joke, bumping her shoulder. "And maybe one stubborn girl who never left my mind."

She smiles, a little shy, a little stronger than she was a few moments ago. "Well. I guess I'm kind of looking forward to meeting this version of you properly."

I grin, holding her gaze. "And I can't wait to get to know this version of you."

She laughs softly, and the sound settles deep in my chest like something sacred.

We stay there a while longer, watching the porch light flicker on, letting the quiet say the rest.

And maybe that's the best part—we don't have to fill every silence.

Sometimes, just sitting here together says everything we need to hear.

We're so wrapped up in our quiet conversation that neither of us notices the sound of a car approaching until headlights sweep across the porch. Annabelle stiffens immediately, her hand tightening in mine.

"Oh no," she whispers nervously, recognizing the vehicle instantly. "It's my dad."

My stomach clenches, heart rate spiking as Mr. Dawson steps out of his car, his face stern and hard-edged with anger. He approaches quickly, his eyes locked onto mine.

"Marcus," he snaps sharply. "What the hell do you think you're doing here?"

I stand up slowly, positioning myself protectively between him and Annabelle, even though I know it'll just make things worse. "We were just talking, sir. That's all."

"Just talking?" He scoffs bitterly. "After I explicitly told you to stay away from my daughter?"

"Dad, stop," Annabelle says quickly, rolling forward. "He hasn't done anything wrong. We're just trying to sort things out."

He turns sharply toward her, voice strained. "Annabelle, you don't understand what kind of trouble he brings."

"I'm right here," I interject, frustration rising. "If you have something to say, say it to me. Leave Annabelle out of it."

Mr. Dawson narrows his eyes, stepping closer until we're almost face-to-face. "You want me to say it to you? Fine. You left once, Marcus, and it nearly destroyed her. Do you think you deserve a second chance after the damage you did?"

His words land like a punch, guilt and anger mingling sharply in my chest. "I know what I did. I regret it every day. But Annabelle deserves to make her own decisions."

"She's not ready for this!" he snaps harshly. "She barely remembers you, and already you're confusing her again. If you care at all, you'll walk away."

My fists clench at my sides, fury and hurt warring inside me. But before I can speak, Annabelle pushes forward firmly.

"Dad, that's enough," she says sharply, surprising us both with her strength. "I'm not a child anymore. Marcus hasn't forced anything on me. He's been patient and respectful. I chose to invite him here."

Mr. Dawson's gaze flickers uncertainly, his anger softening slightly as he looks at his daughter. "Annabelle, I'm just trying to protect you. You don't understand how painful it was—"

"Then help me understand!" she interrupts desperately. "Stop hiding things from me. I need to know everything, not just your version."

He exhales heavily, frustration evident. "Fine. But not tonight." He points a stern finger toward me. "Marcus, stay away from her."

My jaw tightens, but I nod stiffly.

He looks at me a long moment, eyes full of wary suspicion. "And Annabelle—stay away from him until we've talked about everything. There are things you don't remember, things you need to know."

He doesn't wait for our response, turning sharply on his heel and walking back to his car. The tires crunch angrily over gravel as he drives away, leaving tense silence hanging between Annabelle and me.

I glance down at her, frustration and worry making it hard for me to think. "Annabelle, I'm sorry—"

She shakes her head, reaching up to touch my arm gently. "Don't apologize. We both knew this was coming."

I sigh heavily, leaning against the porch rail, heart heavy. "Tomorrow isn't going to be fun."

"No," she agrees softly, eyes filled with determination. "But whatever happens, I'm not backing down. Not this time."

I smile faintly, admiration swelling for her quiet bravery. "Neither am I."

~

The stars are out again tonight, scattered across the sky like someone spilled salt on black velvet. I'm parked by the lake, the same one Annabelle and I used to sneak off to when we wanted quiet. Back then, it was all about possibility. Now? It feels like a reflection.

My hands rest on the steering wheel, unmoving.

Annabelle's been opening up more. Slowly. Gently. Like her heart's learning how to trust again, and some part of it is leaning toward *me*.

Which is terrifying.

Because every time I see her smile at me, every time she lets her guard down just a little, there's this voice in the back of my head whispering:

You don't deserve her.

Maybe it sounds like her father's voice. Maybe it's mine.

Maybe there's not much of a difference.

It was the week before I left for college—right after my knee blew out and everything went sideways. I'd just gotten the final call: no scholarship. No offer. No team. My "big future" had officially crumbled, and all I had left was a bedroom full of trophies that suddenly meant nothing.

Dad came in after dinner, arms crossed like he always was, jaw set in that way that made me feel like I was twelve again.

"So that's it, huh?" he said. "No backup plan?"

I didn't look at him. I didn't say anything.

"You had one job. Keep your grades up. Stay in shape. Be the best. Now what are you gonna be, Marcus? Just some townie with a busted knee and a bad attitude?"

The thing is... I wanted to scream at him. Tell him I *wasn't* just a quarterback. That I could be more if someone —*anyone*—ever believed in me for more than my throwing arm.

But I didn't.

I just let the silence answer for me.

And when he left the room, I remember thinking that maybe I really *wasn't* anything if I wasn't someone's trophy.

Back in the present, I rub a hand down my face and stare out at the still water. My reflection blurs in the windshield—messy hair, tired eyes, too much past behind me, and too much future ahead.

Annabelle's father doesn't trust me. I can see it in his eyes. The way he watches me like I'm still the reckless kid who left without looking back.

And hell, maybe he's not wrong.

I left her. I didn't fight harder when everything fell apart. I let my life get small instead of stepping up.

But the difference now? I *want* to be better. Not just for her—but for *me*. The real question is: can I?

Can I be enough for someone who deserves everything?

I don't have the answer tonight. Not yet. But I do know one thing: I'll fight for us, for what we can become, and for something beautiful between us.

I won't be quitting. On Fairhope.

On her.

And on myself.

FACING THE PAST

Annabelle

The moment Dad walks through the front door, I'm ready for a fight. He went out again after driving Marcus away. Probably he needed time to think. But he's back now, and I'm about to drop the gloves.

Usually, I'm not a confrontational person. I've spent most of my life quietly nodding along, accepting Dad's version of events as the absolute truth. But not tonight. Not when Marcus is involved. Not when there's so much hidden beneath the surface, begging for answers.

"Dad," I say firmly, rolling my chair forward to meet him in the hallway. "We need to talk."

He looks at me, startled by my boldness. "Annabelle, it's late. Maybe we should—"

"No." I interrupt, surprising myself with how steady my voice sounds. "No more putting this off. You owe me an explanation. Why are you so determined to keep Marcus away from me?"

He sighs, rubbing his forehead as if this conversation

alone causes him physical pain. "Annabelle, he's not the kind of person you think he is."

I cross my arms, stubborn and trying to keep my emotions in check. "And how do you know what I think? You've spent years hiding the truth from me, Dad. It stops now."

He looks at me sharply, hurt flashing in his eyes. "Everything I've done has been for your own good, to protect you."

"Protect me from what?" I press harder, my frustration mounting. "From Marcus? From the truth?"

"From both," he snaps, his voice rising in a way I rarely hear. "Marcus was reckless, irresponsible. You don't remember, but before he left town, he was constantly in trouble—skipping classes, partying, dragging you into his mess. He changed you, Annabelle."

I feel a flare of irritation, something protective surging inside me. "Changed me how?"

"You stopped caring about your dreams, your plans," Dad insists, sounding angrier than I've seen him recently... or ever, maybe. "You talked about leaving town with him, ditching your future. Marcus Gray was destroying everything you'd worked for."

I stare at him, stunned. Pieces slowly shift into place, but they don't form the picture Dad's describing. Marcus—the Marcus I know—is patient, kind, thoughtful. Could the Marcus he's describing really be the same person?

"Dad, that doesn't sound like him," I argue, my confusion growing. "Maybe he made mistakes, but he's changed."

Dad shakes his head, eyes flashing with stubborn pride. "People like Marcus don't change, Annabelle. He left once, and he'll leave again. He's selfish. He doesn't know how to stick around."

I'm on the brink of tears. "You don't know that."

He sighs, leaning against the wall, shoulders sagging as though suddenly burdened by the weight of all this. "I know what I saw. After he left, you fell apart. You cried yourself to sleep every night. Your grades slipped. And when I finally got you back on track, you had that accident. It was like fate was determined to punish you for ever caring about him."

His words hit hard, feeling guilty about trying to make him seem like the villain here when he was looking out for me. But beneath that guilt, there's a flicker of anger too. Anger at Dad for making choices for me. Anger at the unfairness of blaming Marcus for my accident, for everything wrong in my life.

"Dad, Marcus didn't cause my accident." I'm not about to budge. "He wasn't even here when it happened."

"He didn't have to be here to break your heart," he counters. "You were distracted, reckless, because of him. And I can't risk that happening again."

"Risk what?" My voice trembles with emotion. "Me being happy? Because that's how Marcus makes me feel. He doesn't make me reckless. He makes me brave."

Dad's eyes widen in surprise, then narrow quickly with frustration. "Annabelle—"

"No, Dad," I say, voice rising louder than I intended. "You're wrong about him. You're wrong about me."

Dad's stunned silence echoes through the house. He stares at me, obviously shocked by my defiance. My heart races, adrenaline pumping. I've never talked to him like this before, and part of me is terrified—but another part feels powerful, strong. Free.

"I'm tired of everyone deciding my life for me," I say, my voice steady again. "Marcus isn't perfect. He admits he's made mistakes. But he's also the only person who's been completely honest with me about them. You keep hiding things, hoping I'll just forget. But I won't."

Dad shakes his head, for the hundredth time, I think, and he looks like he's at boiling point. "Annabelle, you're not thinking clearly. He's manipulating you. Marcus Gray is dangerous—"

"Stop!" I interrupt. "He's not dangerous. He's gentle and honest and respectful. He hasn't pressured me once, even though it would've been easy. The Marcus I know would never deliberately hurt me."

"How do you know?" Dad snaps, desperate. "You barely remember him!"

"I know because my heart does," I say softly, conviction ringing clearly in my words. "I feel it. Every time he's with me, every memory that comes back—it all tells me Marcus cares deeply. And so do I."

Dad visibly flinches, pain crossing his face. He takes a step back. He looks older now, as if he has aged just trying to reason with me. "You don't know what you're saying. You're confused—"

"I'm not confused," I insist. "For the first time since the accident, I feel clear. Marcus didn't destroy me, Dad. Losing him did."

The words hang heavy between us. Dad stares silently, eyes wide with shock and grief. Guilt twists in my chest, but I refuse to back down now.

"I don't want to hurt you," I continue. "But I won't pretend anymore. I can't."

He rubs a hand over his face, looking defeated. "Annabelle, I've tried so hard to keep you safe. Marcus is a risk."

"Maybe he is," I admit, honest and unyielding. "But it's my risk to take."

Dad sighs deeply, his voice weary and resigned. "I'm trying to protect you."

"Protecting me doesn't mean keeping me locked away from life," I whisper, feeling tears sting my eyes. "If you love me, let me make my own choices—even if they scare you."

Dad remains quiet for a long moment before he finally straightens, determination building in his eyes.

"Annabelle, I wish I could trust you on this. But I can't risk it," he says with finality. "If Marcus Gray stays in your life, then… I can't support that."

My heart sinks, a chill settling in my chest. "What are you saying?"

He takes a deep breath, avoiding my eyes. "If you choose Marcus, you're choosing to do it without my blessing. Without my help. You'll have to deal with whatever consequences come with him—alone."

I'm stunned, not able to think for a minute. It takes me a while to fully take in what he said. "You're giving me an ultimatum?"

"I'm giving you clarity. I won't watch you throw your life away again. I love you, Annabelle, but this is a decision you'll have to make yourself."

Tears prick my eyes, frustration, hurt, and anger mingling in a cacophony of chaos. "You're punishing me for choosing someone you don't approve of?"

"I'm protecting you," he assures, sadness etched in his voice. "One day, you'll understand."

He walks away, leaving me sitting there stunned, numb, struggling to catch my breath. My head spins, doubts creeping in quickly. Is Dad right about Marcus? About me? Am I blindly repeating old mistakes, chasing feelings I can't even fully remember?

I glance toward the letter still sitting open on the table beside me—my own handwriting confessing deep, powerful feelings for Marcus. Feelings that still tug at my heart, raw and real. Feelings I can't simply turn off because they scare my father.

But is Marcus worth losing Dad over?

The question sits heavy in my chest, sharp and painful. I lean forward, burying my face in my hands, a whirlpool of chaos forming in my mind.

Tonight, I stood up for Marcus. I stood up for myself. But was it brave—or was it reckless?

And am I strong enough to face the consequences of whatever choice I make next?

The house is quiet, still like when everyone else has moved on from the day, but your thoughts refuse to follow.

I sit in my bedroom, legs curled beneath me on the window seat, blanket wrapped around my shoulders. Toby's asleep near the door, twitching now and then like he's chasing butterflies in his dreams. Lucky him.

Outside, the wind sways the trees gently, brushing against the glass like it's trying to whisper something I can't quite hear.

I press my forehead to the windowpane and close my eyes.

I keep replaying Dad's words in my head.

"If you choose Marcus, you're choosing to do it without my blessing. Without my help. You'll have to deal with whatever consequences come with him—alone."

Again. As if loving Marcus once was a mistake.

I know he means well. He always has. Even when it's come out rough and controlling and far too black-and-white.

After the accident, he was there. Every single day. I don't even remember the crash, but I remember waking up in the hospital with his voice cutting through the fog. Not panicked. Just steady. Calm. Like he'd willed himself into strength just to hold me together.

He read to me at night, even though I wasn't awake

enough to hear. He bought every medical book he could find. Built ramps at home with his own hands. Sat in on every therapy session like he was the one learning to walk again.

He was *there*.

And I know not every daughter gets that.

He was the one constant when the rest of the world blurred and broke.

So why do I feel this ache in my chest now? This sadness, this guilt—this *resentment*?

I want to be angry. I want to yell at him for treating me like a child, for not trusting me to make my own decisions. For thinking I'd be reckless enough to throw my life away over a boy—even if that boy is now a man, I'm pretty sure I'm falling for all over again.

But I also remember how scared he looked when he gave me that ultimatum. Not angry. Not mean.

Scared.

Like he thought I'd choose Marcus and he'd lose me all over again.

And I guess… part of me understands that.

Because he *did* lose me once.

Not in the permanent, tragic sense, thank God, but I was gone. The girl he knew—happy, vibrant, head full of dreams—she vanished after the accident. Replaced by someone quiet. Cautious. Afraid.

He built a world to keep me safe. A little too safe, maybe. But it was all he had to give.

And now, here I am—pulling away. Reaching for someone he doesn't trust, someone who broke my heart once and might do it again.

Someone I believe in anyway.

Marcus.

My gosh, even saying his name feels like a rebellion tonight.

But the truth is—I *do* trust him. Maybe I don't have all the memories yet. Maybe I don't remember every kiss, every fight, every inside joke. But my heart... it remembers the rhythm. The warmth. The *feel* of him.

And that's what makes this so damn hard.

How do you stand between the two people who've loved you most, both fighting for you in their own broken, desperate ways?

How do you choose?

The window fogs a little where my breath hits the glass.

Part of me wants to run into Marcus's arms, let him tell me everything will be okay, that love is enough, and we'll figure it out. And part of me wants to rewind to the safety of six months ago, when things were simple and Dad's overprotectiveness still felt like comfort instead of a cage.

I rub my temples and whisper into the dark, "I wish I didn't have to pick."

But I know better.

Because I'm not a little girl anymore. I'm not a patient stuck in recovery or a daughter waiting for someone else to decide her future.

I'm a woman.

A woman who's still healing, yes—but also one who wants *more*. Who *deserves* more.

I deserve to choose who I love. I deserve to believe in Marcus, even if it scares me. Even if it hurts Dad. Even if it means stepping out of the shadow of the past and into a future that isn't guaranteed.

But God, it *hurts*.

The guilt. The longing. The weight of wanting to make everyone proud while still claiming my own heart.

A single tear slips down my cheek before I can stop it.

I brush it away quickly and lean my head back against the cool glass.

Maybe the answer isn't choosing one or the other.

Maybe it's trusting myself enough to believe I don't have to lose either.

But that's going to take time.

And courage.

And probably a lot more tears.

Still... I think I'm ready to try.

CHOICES AND CONSEQUENCES

Marcus

*W*atching Annabelle's dad lash out at me felt a lot like getting tackled by an entire defensive line. I still feel bruised—on the inside, where it hurts most. After that heated confrontation, Annabelle and I agree silently, exchanging glances that spoke volumes. We both need space to breathe, to process. So I quietly slip away, leaving her with a gentle promise to talk soon.

Now I'm standing at the edge of Fairhope Lake, kicking pebbles into the water like a frustrated teenager. It's ironic how familiar this feels. How many times did I stand here after fights with my dad or a disappointing game? But tonight feels different—heavier. Tonight's stakes are way higher than some stupid Friday night football game.

I stare at the moonlit lake, memories playing through my mind. Annabelle's laughter, the way we talked about everything going on in the town, stolen kisses beneath these same stars. I'd give anything to turn back time, to make different choices—choices that wouldn't have left scars on her heart or mine.

Her father's words keep echoing painfully inside my head. "You left once, and you'll leave again." The worst part is, I get why he thinks that. Hell, part of me even agrees with him. Leaving Annabelle once nearly destroyed her. Could I risk doing that again, even if it means keeping her safe?

My shoulders slump in an involuntary gesture of defeat as I inhale sharply. I can't deny the truth—I'm terrified. I care for Annabelle more deeply now than I ever imagined possible. But what if her dad's right? What if loving me only brings her pain?

Eventually, my phone buzzes in my pocket, jolting me back to reality.

Ethan: Hey, you okay? Heard things got intense. Want to talk?

I exhale, grateful for Ethan's timing. He might not always seem serious, but he's been my rock through more storms than I can count.

Me: Yeah, man. Meet you at your place?

His reply is instant:

Ethan: On my way.

~

Twenty minutes later, I'm sprawled out on Ethan's beat-up couch, staring at his cracked ceiling like it might have answers. Ethan hands me a soda and sits across from me, his expression surprisingly sober.

"So," he begins, cracking open his drink, "you thinking about leaving again?"

The bluntness hits like ice water. "You really don't waste any time, do you?"

"Hey, you know me," he shrugs lightly. "I figure you didn't come here for me to sugarcoat things."

I rub my face, sighing. "I don't know what to do. Her

dad's convinced I'll hurt her again. Maybe he's right. Maybe she's better off without me around."

Ethan raises an eyebrow skeptically. "And you think just disappearing again would solve things? Didn't work out too great the first time, remember?"

I flinch slightly, but I know he's right. "What else am I supposed to do, Ethan? If me staying hurts Annabelle or makes things worse with her dad, how can I justify that?"

He leans forward, fixing me with a look that's far more serious than his usual carefree manner. "Marcus, have you ever stopped to consider that you leaving is what actually hurt Annabelle? Not staying."

I pause, heart tightening. "Of course I have."

Ethan sighs heavily, shaking his head. "Then why consider it again? You've spent so much time worrying about how you might fail, Annabelle, but have you considered how much she's gained from having you back?"

I glance away, uncomfortable with the raw truth in his words. "She barely remembers—"

"Maybe not everything, but have you seen her lately? Really seen her?" Ethan presses. "She's laughing again. She's fighting back against people making decisions for her. That's not just memory, Marcus. That's strength—and you've helped her find that."

My heart hurts, part hope, part fear. "But Ethan, her dad's ultimatum—it's me or him. How can I ask Annabelle to make that choice?"

"You don't." Ethan shrugs, but it's a shrug that doesn't indicate uncertainty. "But you don't get to make it for her, either."

"Then what?"

"You stop running, man," Ethan echoes the voice in my head. "Love isn't easy. Sometimes it means staying put and facing your fears. Annabelle deserves that much from you."

"I know," I admit softly, feeling vulnerable. "But what if I screw this up again? What if her dad's right?"

Ethan gives me a knowing, sympathetic look. "That's the risk you take with love. It's never safe. But when it's real, Marcus, it's always worth it."

I stare down at the cracked linoleum floor, his words sinking deep inside me. Ethan's right. Leaving won't protect Annabelle—it'll only wound her again, deeper this time. Love means taking risks, standing firm even when it scares the hell out of you.

I glance back at Ethan, grateful beyond words. "When did you get so wise?"

He laughs, leaning back casually. "Been spending too much time watching soap operas with my mom, I guess."

I chuckle, feeling a little lighter despite myself. "Thanks, man. I needed this."

"Anytime." Ethan's eyes twinkle with pride. "But Marcus?"

"Yeah?"

"Don't run this time," he says, dead serious. "She deserves better."

"I know," I promise. "I'm done running."

I don't sleep much that night, tossing restlessly, replaying Ethan's advice and Annabelle's dad's warnings over and over. By morning, I'm wired and restless, anxious for clarity, desperate to talk to Annabelle.

As I'm pouring coffee, my phone buzzes loudly. My heart jolts when I see Annabelle's name flash across the screen.

I quickly open the message, pulse racing:

Annabelle: Left something for you on your porch. Please read it.

Confused, I step outside quickly. A small envelope rests against the railing, the handwriting instantly recognizable. I open it slowly, heart hammering as I read:

Marcus,

I spent all night thinking. About you, about us, about everything my dad said. I need clarity, and I think you do too.

Can we meet later? Just us, somewhere quiet? We need to talk about what comes next. I don't want any more secrets, any more half-truths. Whatever happens, we face it together.

If you're willing, meet me by our old sugar mill spot at sunset.

Yours,

A

P.S. I'm writing this letter instead of texting because something tells me we used to do this as teens. Did I remember it correctly?

I stare at her letter, and my mind time travels back to our teenage years...

We were juniors. Barely old enough to know what we were doing, but already way too deep to pretend it didn't matter.

Annabelle had this thing she did. Notes. Not the folded-square, pass-it-in-class kind of letters. Sweet, cutesy, handwritten letters on lined notebook paper, complete with curly arrows and sometimes doodles of hearts in the margins. She'd tuck them in my locker, in my hoodie pocket, once even in the back of my playbook.

Always signed the same way:

– Yours. A.

At first, I didn't know what to actually do with them.

I was Marcus Gray—Fairhope's golden boy. Quarterback. Kind-of-a-jerk heartthrob. I didn't write letters. I barely even responded to texts with full words. Everything about me had to scream cool, detached, unbothered.

So the first few times, I didn't write back.

Didn't say anything.

I'd read them in private, tucked away in my truck or during practice breaks when no one was looking. And I'd smile like a fool. Sometimes I'd reread them twice. Three times. Memorize little phrases like she'd written them in some secret code meant only for me.

But then I'd show up at school and nod at her like nothing happened. Play it chill. Like I was the one doing her a favor by letting her sit beside me at lunch or wearing her bracelet tucked under my sleeve.

What a punk.

But the thing is... she never stopped.

And each note chipped at me a little more. Softened the edges. Made me want to stop being cool long enough to be hers—out loud, in public, no pretending.

One afternoon, she slipped a note through the vents of my locker. I still remember exactly what it said.

You looked tired today. I hope you're sleeping okay. If not, imagine the stars tucking you in, one by one. They told me you dream in touchdowns and terrible jokes. I told them they weren't wrong.

P.S. If you ever write me back, I'll probably faint.

– Yours. A.

I stood there staring at it like it was some ancient text I had to decode.

And then I cracked.

That night, I pulled out one of my spiral notebooks and tore a page from the middle. My handwriting was awful. The lines were crooked. The pen smudged at least twice. But I wrote her back.

I don't dream in touchdowns. I dream in your laugh.

You're the only thing that makes the noise shut up

Don't faint.

– M.

I folded it four times and shoved it into her locker the next morning before homeroom. Then I spent the entire day avoiding eye contact because I felt like I'd handed her my entire soul on a piece of lined paper.

That night, she sent me a voice message of her laughing—just laughing.

And I swear, I replayed that dumb thing like it was a song.

After that, it became our thing.

Notes tucked into books and glove compartments. Scribbled corners of napkins at the diner. Once, she left one under the windshield wiper of my truck during a rainstorm—it bled ink everywhere, but I kept it anyway. Still have it, somewhere in a box marked "old stuff" that I haven't opened in years.

She never needed paragraphs. Her words always found the part of me I didn't show anyone else.

And I—I didn't have the language for love yet. But she gave me the alphabet. The grammar. The safety to even try.

The memories make me smile. I'm feeling more hopeful than I've been in a while. Annabelle is slowly starting to remember. It might be a long process, but... she might start to remember us, remember what we had.

Her courage amazes me—despite everything, she's choosing honesty, even when it's terrifying. She's right; it's time we stop running from our past and start confronting our future.

Ethan's words ring true in my ears again, stronger this time. "Love means facing your fears."

Clutching her note, I look toward the rising sun, determined. Tonight, we'll finally lay everything out. No secrets, no hiding.

It's a risk, sure—but Annabelle Dawson is worth every ounce of it. And this time, I won't let anything—fear, doubt, or even her father—stand in the way.

THE HEART'S DILEMMA

Annabelle

*I*t's funny how certain moments make your life feel like it's hanging in the balance. Tonight, standing near the old sugar mill, I know I'm about to make one of those decisions. Marcus isn't here yet, and the silence feels thick around me, filled with possibilities—some good, some scary, some utterly unpredictable.

I let out a shaky breath, tugging my sweater tighter as I watch the fading sunset paint streaks of lavender and gold across the sky. This was our place once—a spot hidden enough for whispered secrets and stolen moments, back when we believed we could hide forever from the real world. Now, it's where we'll decide whether our past still has room in our future.

Headlights flicker through the trees, pulling me from my thoughts. Marcus's truck pulls in slowly, gravel crunching softly beneath the tires. My heart speeds up—nerves, excitement, fear. I can't pinpoint exactly what I'm feeling. Maybe it's everything all at once.

He steps out of the truck, looking as nervous as I feel.

But beneath that anxiousness, there's warmth in his eyes—a kind of gentle strength that always seems to calm my fears.

"Hey," Marcus says quietly, approaching me slowly, hands tucked in his pockets.

"Hey, yourself," I reply softly, offering a small smile.

He stops a few feet away, as though unsure if he should come closer. "Thanks for leaving the note. You okay?"

I nod slowly, breathing out carefully. "I think so. But honestly, my nerves are shot."

Marcus chuckles lightly, visibly relaxing. "Yeah, I get that. Mine too."

We fall quiet for a moment, the rustle of leaves and the distant hum of crickets filling the silence. Finally, Marcus gestures gently toward our familiar spot near the old oak tree.

"Wanna sit down?" he asks softly. "Feels like this conversation might take a while."

"Good idea," I whisper, relieved. He helps me to our spot beneath the massive oak, its branches spreading wide, protective and comforting overhead. Marcus settles onto the grass beside me, and for a long moment, neither of us speaks. We just sit quietly, absorbing the peacefulness around us.

"I missed this," Marcus finally says quietly, gazing up at the tree.

"Me too," I admit softly. "Even when I couldn't remember clearly, it felt like part of me was missing. Now I realize it was you."

Marcus turns toward me, surprise and tenderness clear in his eyes. "Annabelle, you don't have to—"

"I mean it," I interrupt gently. "The last few days, seeing you, remembering pieces of us…it feels like finally coming home. But it scares me too."

Marcus exhales, relief mingling with understanding.

"Me too. Your dad made some good points. I did hurt you back then. Leaving was the worst choice I've ever made."

I shake my head slowly. "You keep carrying that guilt, Marcus. But you were young. We both were. Mistakes happen, right?"

"Yeah," he says softly, glancing down. "But some mistakes cost more than others."

I reach out instinctively, touching his hand softly. His warmth sends a comforting shiver through me. "Maybe, but I've learned something. Sometimes mistakes teach us the most about ourselves."

Marcus glances up again, searching my face. "What's this one taught you?"

I smile softly. "That second chances exist, and they're worth fighting for. But I don't want us to keep hiding from truths or tiptoeing around each other."

Marcus's lips curve into a tender smile. "You're braver than I'll ever be."

"Not brave, just tired of being cautious," I whisper. "I spent so long hiding behind what other people thought was best for me. My dad means well, but he's not always right. I need to live for myself."

Marcus nods slowly, understanding deepening in his gaze. "So where does that leave us?"

I squeeze his hand gently. "Right here, figuring it out together."

Marcus and I sit quietly again, the evening air cooling around us, but I barely notice. My heart feels warm, full of new possibilities. Still, one question lingers—an uncertainty I can't quite ignore.

"Marcus?" I ask quietly, glancing toward him. "Did you read my letter more than once?"

He chuckles softly, squeezing my hand lightly. "Only about fifty times."

"Good," I smile gently. "Because every word was true.

Even though I can't fully remember writing it, I feel it all. Especially the part about how you always made me braver. You still do."

Marcus exhales softly, visibly touched. "Annabelle, back then, you were the only person who really knew me—the only one I trusted. Losing you wasn't just painful. It was like losing a part of myself."

I swallow hard, feeling his sincerity deeply. "I think that's why this feels so right. Because deep down, we never fully lost each other, did we?"

"No," he whispers gently. "We just took a long, painful detour."

I laugh softly, appreciating his honesty. "Let's avoid those from now on, okay?"

Marcus smiles warmly, eyes tender. "Deal. No more detours."

We fall quiet again, comfortable now, content to simply be close. My heart feels lighter, clearer than it has in days. I realize something important: I don't want to live carefully anymore. I want authenticity, honesty, even if it means taking risks.

"You know," Marcus says suddenly, breaking the quiet, "Ethan said something earlier. He told me love means facing your fears and sticking around, no matter how hard it gets. I think he might've been talking sense for once."

I smile gently, squeezing his hand again. "He's smarter than we give him credit for."

"Yeah," Marcus admits quietly. "I guess I just never thought about love that way until now."

My heart skips, suddenly nervous and hopeful. "And now?"

He meets my eyes seriously, vulnerable but determined. "Now, I know it's true. Love isn't just easy or simple. But if it's real, it's worth fighting for. And Annabelle, nothing's ever felt as real as you."

My breath catches softly, eyes filling with sudden tears. "Marcus, you're making me emotional."

He smiles sheepishly, squeezing my hand. "Sorry. I tend to do that."

"Don't apologize," I whisper, leaning closer. "I just...I never thought I'd feel this sure about anything again. Especially about you."

Marcus smiles softly, the warmth of his gaze almost overwhelming. "Then maybe we finally got something right."

"Maybe we did," I agree, resting my head gently on his shoulder, feeling utterly safe for the first time in ages.

We stay beneath our oak tree, feeling a lot lighter after confiding in each other honestly, watching stars slowly brighten overhead. I know our conversation is far from finished—my dad's warnings still echo faintly in the back of my mind—but right now, sitting here with Marcus feels like exactly where I'm supposed to be.

Yet, one nagging question still tugs at my thoughts—a puzzle piece that doesn't quite fit. Finally, I lift my head, turning to Marcus again.

"Marcus?" I ask quietly, catching his attention.

"Yeah?" he replies softly, meeting my gaze gently.

"There's something I still don't understand." I pause, gathering my courage. "You could've gone anywhere after your injury. You had plenty of places, opportunities, people waiting for you. But you chose to come back here—to Fairhope. Why?"

Marcus hesitates, clearly taken aback. His eyes grow thoughtful, and I sense how important his next words will be.

"That's the real question, isn't it?" he murmurs finally, smiling gently at me.

"Yeah," I whisper, feeling vulnerable again. "Why come back to a place filled with painful memories and people who judge you?"

He takes a deep breath, holding my gaze steady. "Because, Annabelle, no matter where I went, I couldn't shake the feeling that I'd left something important behind. Something I'd never find anywhere else."

My heart pounds gently, waiting for him to finish.

Marcus reaches up softly, tucking a stray strand of hair behind my ear, his touch gentle and full of quiet sincerity.

"That something important was you," he whispers, voice thick with emotion. "Fairhope isn't home because of football or childhood memories. It's home because of you. And I finally realized I couldn't stay away any longer."

His words ripple through me, sending warmth deep into my bones, filling my heart with clarity. I stare at Marcus, stunned into silence, my breath caught in my chest, afraid yet exhilarated by what his words could mean.

The answer was exactly what I'd hoped—but hearing it out loud feels like crossing a bridge, with no going back. I believe he has a lot more to say, which he makes clear by the way he's looking at me, and even though I'm not sure what exactly I can expect, I know the connection between us is growing stronger.

TRUTHS REVEALED

Marcus

I hold Annabelle's gaze, my confession making the atmosphere around us suddenly seem very tense. It's out now, every hidden truth I've carried since the moment I came back to Fairhope.

"You came back...for me?" she whispers softly, her voice barely audible over the gentle rustling of the leaves overhead.

"Yeah," I admit quietly, giving a small shrug, though it feels like the understatement of the century. "At first, I convinced myself it was just about closure. I told myself I needed to come back, face all the mess I left behind, find some way to move on. But deep down, I always knew it was about you. It's always been about you."

She blinks slowly, her eyes glistening, reflecting a mixture of surprise and something deeper. Her lips part as though she wants to speak, but nothing comes out. That silence nearly kills me.

"You don't have to say anything," I quickly assure her. "I just needed you to know the truth—why I'm really here. And why, no matter what happens, I'm not leaving again."

Annabelle draws a shaky breath and then slowly reaches out, lacing her fingers through mine. Her touch sends warmth directly to my heart.

"I never thought I'd hear you say that," she admits, eyes dropping to our entwined hands. "You always seemed so sure of yourself back then, so ready to leave Fairhope behind."

I chuckle softly, shaking my head. "I was pretending, Annabelle. The truth is, I had no clue who I was or what I wanted. All I knew was that you deserved better. But running away didn't fix anything—it just made it worse."

She lifts her gaze again, searching my eyes carefully, as though looking for the hidden lies or half-truths I once fed her. But there are none left.

"You know," she whispers gently, almost shyly, "you keep talking about how much you hurt me. But since you've been back, you've made me stronger, braver, even happier. Maybe you need to forgive yourself, Marcus."

I breathe out slowly, touched beyond words by her quiet strength. "I'm trying. But seeing you struggle, knowing I caused some of that pain—it's hard to let go of that guilt."

Annabelle squeezes my hand lightly, her touch reassuring. "We're both different people now. Stronger. Wiser, maybe. At least a little."

I smile faintly, nodding. "Definitely wiser. At least you are. Jury's still out on me."

She laughs softly, the sound warm and bright, cutting through the tension. "Well, you're wiser than you give yourself credit for. After all, you found your way back."

"Yeah," I murmur quietly, holding her gaze. "Took me long enough."

We both grow silent again, perhaps thinking that a

prolonged conversation could destroy the sanctity of this moment. As twilight deepens, the gentle glow of stars begins appearing overhead. I glance at Annabelle again, happier than I've been in months—no, years. No matter how uncertain the future is, right now, in this moment, nothing feels clearer than my love for her.

~

We stay beneath the old oak for a long while, neither of us eager to break the quiet peace we've found. But eventually, Annabelle shifts slightly, turning toward me with a more serious expression.

"Marcus," she says softly, hesitantly, "there's still something I have to deal with. My dad isn't going to back down easily."

I nod slowly, understanding why she sounds so worried. *Of course she has to consider her father's dim view of me.* "Yeah, I know. But whatever happens with him, you don't have to face it alone. I'll be right here."

She bites her lip nervously, looking away. "I appreciate that, but he gave me an ultimatum. He said I have to choose—either him or you."

It's painful to hear her say that, but I force myself to remain steady. "Annabelle, I want you to know something important. If it ever comes down to making that choice, don't pick me out of guilt or obligation. Pick what your heart needs. Whatever you decide, I'll respect it."

She meets my gaze sharply, eyes wide with surprise. "You really mean that, don't you?"

"I do," I whisper seriously. "Your happiness matters more than my own, Annabelle. I learned that the hard way, but now I know what love really means. It's not selfish. It's putting someone else first."

Her eyes soften, filled with warmth and gratitude. "I think that's the sweetest thing you've ever said to me."

I grin sheepishly, shrugging lightly. "Yeah, well, don't spread it around. I still have a tough-guy reputation to uphold."

Annabelle laughs softly again, easing some of the lingering tension. "Your secret's safe with me."

We spend some quiet moments, but soon Annabelle sighs softly, clearly struggling internally. "Marcus, part of me knows you're right—that love should mean choosing happiness over fear. But there's another part that's still afraid. My dad's approval means more to me than I ever realized. I don't want to lose him, even if I know he's wrong about us."

I squeeze her hand again gently, meeting her gaze with a seriousness that suggests I mean every word I say. "I get it. Family's complicated. I never had the best relationship with my dad either. But you're strong enough to handle this, Annabelle, however it works out."

"Am I?" she whispers, voice uncertain.

"Absolutely," I reassure her firmly. "You've already proven it, facing down your dad, confronting me, pushing through your memory loss. That's strength."

She smiles faintly, but the uncertainty still clouds her eyes. "I just wish I knew the right decision."

"You'll know," I promise quietly. "Trust your heart. It hasn't failed you yet."

She exhales softly, relaxing slightly again. "Thank you, Marcus. You always seem to know just what I need to hear."

"Lucky guess," I joke gently, nudging her shoulder playfully.

Annabelle chuckles softly, eyes brightening again. "Maybe."

We linger just a bit longer, unwilling to leave each

other's company and the promises we just made. But eventually, night falls fully, stars filling the darkened sky. Annabelle shivers lightly in the cool air, and I reluctantly realize it's time to head back.

"Come on," I say softly, standing up and offering my hand. "Let's get you home."

She hesitates only a second before taking it, her fingers warm in mine. "Thanks, Marcus. For everything tonight."

"Anytime," I reply gently, meaning every word.

The drive home is quiet but comfortable, each of us lost in thought. As we pull into Annabelle's driveway, the lights from the house glow softly, and suddenly, a tension fills the car again.

"Guess it's back to reality," Annabelle whispers softly, glancing toward the house.

I nod, offering an encouraging smile. "You've got this. And remember, whatever happens, I'm here."

She smiles. "Thanks, Marcus. I'll remember."

We sit quietly for another moment, neither eager to say goodbye. Finally, Annabelle's phone vibrates loudly in her pocket, breaking the silence.

She pulls it out quickly, eyes narrowing in concern as she reads the message. Her face pales slightly, worry filling her gaze.

"Everything okay?" I ask, trying to sound as calm as possible.

"It's my dad," she replies, nervousness clear in her voice, and shows me the screen. The message is brief, blunt, urgent:

We need to talk immediately. Family meeting at home. Now.

I sense trouble ahead, but don't let her catch on to my anxiety. "You think it's about us?"

She sighs heavily, nodding. "I'm sure of it."

"Do you want me to come with you?" I offer gently.

Annabelle hesitates, considering, then shakes her head. "No, this is something I have to face alone. But Marcus?"

"Yeah?"

"Whatever happens, promise you'll be here afterward?" she whispers.

I reach out, gently brushing her cheek with my thumb, eyes full of sincerity. "Always."

She smiles faintly, exhaling slowly as she prepares to leave the car. "Wish me luck."

"You don't need it," I say, making sure my voice remains warm despite the turmoil in my head. "You've got this."

As I watch her wheel herself toward the front door, my heart twists painfully, torn between pride at her courage and fear for what's to come.

Whatever happens inside that house tonight will determine our future—hers, mine, maybe ours. But as I promised her, no matter what comes next, *I'll be right here, waiting*.

Annabelle deserves that much—and so much more.

FAMILY TIES

Annabelle

*D*ad's standing in the doorway like he gets to decide when the room stops being silent.

He's not saying anything yet, which is somehow worse than if he'd come in yelling. His arms are crossed, his mouth set in that same tight line he gets when he's holding back too much.

I sit on the edge of the couch, blanket half over my lap, fingers tangled around the hem like I'm thirteen again and in trouble for sneaking out. Which is ridiculous because I'm not a kid anymore. And this—this isn't about a missed curfew. This is about *me*.

About Marcus.

"You've been spending a lot of time with him," Dad finally says, voice low and careful.

I nod, even though I already know where this is going. "Yeah. I have."

He exhales through his nose, slow and long, like I've just confirmed his worst fear. "Annabelle... I know what you think you're doing. I know how it looks—romantic, exciting. But you're letting emotions cloud your judgment."

I blink. "Judgment?" My voice cracks just a little. "Dad, he's not a criminal. He's Marcus."

"He's also the boy who left you when things got hard."

"And now he's the man who came back."

That catches him off guard. He looks at me like he's trying to figure out when exactly I started answering back. I don't usually push. I've spent most of the past two years letting him lead the way. Letting him decide what's safe, what's smart, what's best for me.

But I can't do that anymore. Not when I finally feel like I'm breathing again.

Dad steps into the room, slowly, like he's still trying to keep things calm. "Belle, sweetheart, I'm not saying this to hurt you. I just… I know how fragile everything is. You've come so far. Your therapy, your recovery—it took everything. Do you really want to risk all that for someone who's already let you down once?"

I swallow hard, because yeah, that part still hurts.

It *did* wreck me when Marcus left. Even if I don't remember the moment itself, I remember the hollow. The missing. The way my heart seemed to know something was gone long before my mind caught up.

"I don't feel fragile anymore," I say quietly.

Dad sighs. "I know you want to feel strong. I want that for you too. But wanting it doesn't mean you're ready."

I let the blanket fall from my lap and sit up straighter. "But you don't get to decide what I'm ready for."

He flinches. Just a little. Just enough that I know the words hit.

"I've been rebuilding my life," I go on, voice shaking, but not from weakness. "And yeah, it's been hard. And messy. And slow. But Marcus makes me feel like myself again. Not just the girl in the chair. Not just your patient. He remembers the *whole* me. Even the parts I've forgotten."

Dad looks at me, and for the first time, I think I see fear in his eyes instead of anger.

"I'm scared," he says softly. "Is that so hard to understand?"

"No," I whisper. "It's not."

Because I'm scared too.

Scared of falling. Of remembering things that hurt. Of believing in someone who once walked away.

But I'm more scared of staying small. Of locking myself in a life that's safe but lonely. Of being so protected, I forget what it feels like to *live*.

"I don't want to be alone forever," I say, more to myself than him. "I know you think I've got everything I need here. But love isn't a luxury, Dad. It's part of healing too. And I deserve that."

There's a long, heavy pause between us.

His jaw flexes, like he's biting back a dozen arguments, but he doesn't say them. Maybe because he knows I won't back down. Not this time.

He nods once. A stiff, reluctant sort of nod. Then he steps back toward the doorway.

"I'll always be here," he says quietly. "Even when you think you don't need me."

"I know," I whisper.

And I do.

But I also know that being here doesn't mean holding me back.

Sometimes love means letting go of control.

And I think we're both learning that.

It's strange, the things that stick with you.

Like I can't remember my first kiss with Marcus, but I remember what it felt like the first time someone looked at me like I was broken.

It was a month after I got home from the hospital. I'd gone to the grocery store with Dad, trying to do something *normal*. I remember how heavy the air felt, how every sound echoed too loudly in my ears. My hands wouldn't stop shaking on the cart.

Dad had stepped away for a minute to grab something. I was parked near the produce, trying to decide whether I wanted strawberries or just to go home. That's when I heard it.

A woman—not much older than me, maybe mid-twenties—whispered too loudly to her friend, "It's such a shame. She's so pretty… but, you know."

That *pause*.

A type of pause that says more than the words ever could.

But, you know.

Like being in a wheelchair somehow canceled out the rest of me.

I didn't cry. Not there. Not in public. I just turned and stared at the apples until they left. I don't even remember what I bought. I just remember feeling like I was no longer a whole person. Like I was reduced to a chair with a face.

That feeling—that *weight*—sat with me for a long time.

Sometimes, it still does.

Tonight, it sits heavier than usual.

Dad's gone to bed. The house is quiet. And I'm back in my room, curled up in the same window seat where I once promised myself I'd never let anyone make me feel small again.

But now… I'm scared.

Not of Dad's words. I've heard his warnings before, even if this one came wrapped as an ultimatum.

I'm scared of what happens if he's right.

What if I let myself fall all the way for Marcus—*really* fall—and then one day he looks at me and sees someone who can't do everything? Someone who needs help more often than she wants to admit? Someone who doesn't match the version of love he used to know?

What if he gets tired?

What if I'm *too much* and *not enough* all at once?

I squeeze my eyes shut and press my forehead to the cool glass. My heart beats too loud in the silence. I don't want to doubt him. He's done nothing but show up, again and again, no matter how hard I've tried to push him away.

But those fears—they don't listen to logic.

They whisper.

They *linger*.

And still… something deeper in me rises up. A steadier voice.

Marcus isn't that girl in the produce aisle. He's never looked at me like I'm less than. He's never hesitated to hold my hand or meet my eyes or ask me questions no one else had the patience to ask.

He sees me.

Even before I see myself.

Maybe that's why this whole thing matters so much.

Not because I want to prove something to my father. Not even because I need Marcus to fill some missing piece.

But because I'm slowly finding those pieces on my own. In bits of memory. In small steps. In the way my heart races when I see a flash of who I used to be—who I *still am*.

I reach for the little box of mementos I've been keeping under my bed. It's full of randomness—pages from sketchbooks, a concert ticket I found in my old coat pocket, a bracelet I don't remember buying but somehow can't throw away.

I dig until I find the photo again.

Marcus and me.

Laughing.

Free.

And I realize—I owe it to her. The girl in that picture. I owe it to *me*.

To make peace with these memories. Not just the ones that hurt, but the ones that made me feel whole. The ones that shaped me before the world cracked open beneath my feet.

If I want this—*really* want a future with Marcus—I can't just hope the past stays buried. I have to unearth it. Look it in the eye.

Even if it's messy. Even if it stings.

Because maybe, healing doesn't mean forgetting everything that broke me.

Maybe it means picking up the pieces, one at a time, and choosing to keep them.

BRIDGING THE GAP

Marcus

*W*hen I wake up, it's like something clicks into place.

No more waiting around, hoping fate works its magic and fixes the mess I helped make. It's on me now. If I want Annabelle to remember who she is—who *we* were—then I need to do something about it. Starting today.

And yeah, organizing a surprise get-together in Fairhope, the town where secrets have a shelf life of five minutes? Nearly impossible. But somehow, I pull it off. Mostly thanks to Ethan, who's always been better at whispering rumors than actually keeping them.

Now I'm standing in his backyard under a mess of string lights, surrounded by familiar faces I haven't seen since graduation. It feels... weirdly good. For a while, I didn't think I belonged here anymore. But right now? It feels like maybe I never really left.

There's Abby, who used to braid Annabelle's hair in study hall like it was an Olympic event. Charlie's here too, grinning like always—the guy could make Annabelle laugh even when everything sucked. And Sarah, of course, who still holds the Fairhope record for most hours spent gossiping at the diner.

Ethan claps a hand on my shoulder and hands me a soda. "Gotta admit, man. I didn't think you had this kind of sentimental drama in you."

"Yeah, well," I shrug, scanning the crowd, "she deserves it. She needs to see pieces of who she was. People who actually remember her."

Ethan smirks, sipping his drink. "Marcus Gray: small-town heartthrob turned emotional support quarterback. Who would've guessed?"

"Let's keep that nickname between us, yeah?" I nudge him, laughing. "I still have a reputation to ruin slowly."

Before he can hit me with another comeback, head-lights sweep across the backyard, lighting up the fence and kicking my heartbeat into overdrive.

She's here.

Ethan heads off to meet her, and I stay planted under the lights, trying not to look like a guy who's about to throw up.

Annabelle rolls in beside him, eyes wide, taking in the crowd. She looks confused—okay, *really* confused—but not upset. More... overwhelmed in that good, kind of way. The kind of overwhelmed you feel when something soft cracks open in your chest.

Her eyes find mine almost instantly.

"Marcus... what is all this?"

I walk over slowly, hands jammed in my pockets, and give her a smile I hope looks cooler than I feel. "Thought maybe you'd like to see some old faces. Give your memory a little nudge."

She looks around, really taking it in this time—the friends, the lights, the way everyone's smiling like this is some magical time warp back to the best version of Fairhope. Her eyes start to glisten.

"You did this for me?"

I nod, suddenly sheepish. "Yeah. Ethan helped. But... yeah. You deserve this, Annabelle."

The way she looks at me—like I just gave her back a piece of herself—nearly levels me.

"Thank you," she says, and her voice is so soft I almost miss it.

"Come on," I grin, holding out my hand. "There are some people here who've been waiting a long time to see you."

She takes my hand—no hesitation—and squeezes. "Let's go."

The next hour is something I won't forget anytime soon.

Annabelle comes alive in a way I haven't seen since I came back. The uncertainty melts off her face as she reconnects with Abby, laughs with Charlie, listens to Sarah's dramatic retellings of diner drama from ten years ago. It's like each moment puts a puzzle piece back where it belongs.

And from my spot near the fire pit, I just watch. Let it soak in. Her laugh rings out across the backyard, and for the first time in a long time, I feel like I did something right.

Ethan elbows me, smug. "Still think this wasn't a genius idea?"

I roll my eyes, chuckling. "Fine. You get partial credit."

As the party winds down, Annabelle wheels herself over, cheeks flushed and eyes brighter than I've ever seen them.

"This was amazing," she says. "I don't even know how to thank you."

"You don't have to," I tell her. "Just seeing you like this? That's more than enough."

Her smile fades just a little—turns thoughtful. "Tonight helped fill in gaps I didn't even know were there. Every hug, every old story—it brought pieces of me back."

"Yeah?" I ask, heart thudding. "Like what?"

She looks down, a little bashful. "Like you always saving me your fries at lunch. Like sneaking away during pep rallies to draw by the lake. Like how Abby used to cover for us even though we were absolutely *terrible* at sneaking out."

I laugh. "Ethan always knew, too."

"Oh, *everyone* knew," she says, grinning. "But we didn't care. Back then, it felt like we had the whole world."

"We did," I murmur, and it slips out before I can stop it.

She doesn't look away. "You know... I think I'm finally ready to make a real decision about my life. And I want you in it."

My chest tightens, in the best way. I kneel beside her chair and meet her eyes.

"I'll be here. Whatever you decide. I'm not going anywhere."

She nods, eyes shining. "Good. Because I'm tired of letting fear decide everything. I want to live again. Not just exist."

I brush a thumb across her hand. "You deserve all of it."

She reaches up and cups my cheek, her touch light but steady. "And so do you, Marcus."

Most of the guests have trickled out. Ethan's collecting cups and humming something that sounds suspiciously like a wedding march. Annabelle and I sit in the quiet glow of the string lights, fingers still tangled.

She sighs, content. "I didn't expect this tonight. But it was exactly what I needed."

"I'm glad," I whisper.

There's a beat of silence. A perfect, stretched-out moment. And then—

Her phone buzzes.

The sound slices through everything like a blade. She glances at the screen, and her whole expression shifts.

"What is it?" I ask, already knowing it's not good.

She turns the screen toward me.

Dad: Annabelle, I heard about tonight. We might have to talk about this.

She doesn't say anything for a second, just keeps holding my hand like it's anchoring her. I see the fear flash in her eyes—but there's something else, too.

Resolve.

"We'll figure it out," I say quietly.

She nods once, eyes locked on mine. "Together?"

"Together."

And this time, I mean it with everything I have.

The diner smells like bacon grease and burnt coffee, which is exactly how I remember it.

Dad's already there when I walk in, sitting in his usual booth like no time has passed at all. He's got the paper folded in front of him, even though I'm pretty sure he's just pretending to read. Same cup of black coffee. Same scowl that doubles as a neutral expression.

I slide into the booth across from him.

He glances up once. "You're late."

"It's 6:02."

"That's still late."

Classic.

I don't answer right away. The silence stretches. I fiddle with the sugar packets on the table, line them up, mess them up again. He watches without commenting.

Finally, I say, "Thanks for agreeing to meet."

Dad nods once, no real expression. "You said it was important."

"It is."

Another long pause. He takes a sip of coffee like it's bracing him for whatever disappointment I'm about to drop.

I inhale, steady and slow. "I wanted to talk about… us. About how things were. And maybe how they could be."

His jaw tightens. "What's there to talk about? You had everything lined up, Marcus. Full ride. Pro scouts. You had the kind of future most kids would kill for."

"I know," I say quietly. "Trust me, I've replayed it more times than I can count."

He nods like that's the only part he needed to hear.

"I just—I guess I wanted you to know I'm not stuck anymore. That I've been working on building something that matters. Coaching. Community stuff. I'm figuring it out."

He doesn't look impressed. "You think that makes up for what you threw away?"

I blink. "I didn't *throw* anything away, Dad. My knee gave out. Life changed. That's not the same thing."

His mouth flattens. "You gave up."

There it is.

That sentence again.

I bite down on the first three things I want to say. I'm not here to argue. I'm here to try.

"I didn't know how to ask for help," I admit instead. "And yeah, I probably shut down. I was eighteen. I didn't have a blueprint for how to survive after losing everything I thought made me... *me*."

Dad leans back, arms crossed. "You could've come home. Stuck it out. You didn't have to run."

"I *did* come home," I say, voice sharper than I mean it to be. "Eventually. And I'm trying now. To fix what I broke. To rebuild something real. I just hoped you'd want to be part of that."

He doesn't respond right away.

The waitress brings more coffee. Neither of us touches it.

Finally, he says, "So what—you come back, pick up a girl you left behind, and now everything's magically better?"

My hands tighten around my mug. "No. But maybe it's *better because I'm finally showing up*. For her. For myself."

Dad snorts softly, not cruelly, just... tired. "That girl— Annabelle. She's been through a lot."

"I know," I say softly. "And I'm not here to save her. She doesn't need saving. But she *does* make me want to be the kind of man I never knew how to be back then."

He studies me for a moment. Doesn't say anything. But he doesn't scoff either, and weirdly, that feels like progress.

We sit in silence for a while. The air's heavy, but not hostile. Just... full of everything unsaid.

"I don't know if I can forget what was lost," he says finally, voice low.

"I'm not asking you to forget," I say. "I'm just asking you to *see* me now. Not the kid with a busted knee. Not the failure. Just... me."

He looks at me for a long second.

Then nods.

Not much.

But enough.

Back outside, the air feels clearer. I don't know what I expected—some kind of tearful reunion? A handshake? A "Son, I'm proud of you"?

Yeah, no. This isn't a movie.

But maybe it's the start of something. A shift. Even a small one.

And I think with Annabelle beside me, I might actually be brave enough to face the rest.

The past doesn't have to be a wall. It can be a foundation.

I just have to keep building.

FACING FORWARD

Annabelle

*L*ying here, staring at the ceiling, I'm replaying the memories from Ethan's backyard party. It feels like every laugh, every familiar face, every comforting hug nudged something loose inside me, coaxing buried feelings out from wherever they'd been hiding.

I smile softly, warmth flooding through my chest as Marcus's face fills my thoughts again. It's strange—bits of my past are still hazy, yet my heart seems to recognize Marcus perfectly.

I don't remember every conversation we had or all the moments we spent together, or even the way he left... but one thing is crystal clear now: I was completely, desperately in love with him back then. And that feeling, somehow, never faded.

It only grew stronger in his absence.

It's scary, knowing this man has the power to shatter me again, but it's even scarier imagining my future without him. Marcus said he wouldn't run this time—and deep down, I know he meant it.

Rolling myself over to the window, I stare out into the quiet street, imagining a future with Marcus by my side. Walks by the lake, drawing sketches of us beneath the old oak tree, lazy mornings filled with laughter, warmth, and adorable chaos. It feels too perfect—like tempting fate—but I don't care. Maybe life owes me a little perfection after everything.

My mind goes into a tizzy as I realize I'm already picturing Marcus in my future, not just today or tomorrow —but years from now. It's thrilling, terrifying, and utterly right. Though my mind might still be trying to rationalize and point out what can go wrong, my heart is dancing in a frenzy of happiness.

The only obstacle now is Dad.

My phone buzzes, and I glance down, half expecting it's Marcus checking in again. But my heart stutters when I see the message is from Dad instead:

Can you meet me on the porch? I'd like to talk.

My anxiety skyrockets, making my hands sweat like crazy. We hadn't spoken the other night because I was tired, and he let it go. Today's the real deal, then.

"Here goes nothing," I whisper softly, rolling myself toward the door.

I spot Dad sitting on the front porch steps, elbows on his knees, staring out across the yard like he's waiting for something that won't come. He doesn't look angry—not like before—but he doesn't look happy either. Somewhere in between. Tired. Worn down. Maybe just… done fighting.

Maybe I am too.

"Hey," I say as I roll up beside him, my voice barely above a whisper. "You wanted to talk?"

He glances over his shoulder, gives me a small smile that doesn't quite reach his eyes. "Yeah. Sit with me a minute?"

I park my chair next to him, close but not too close, and wait. The air between us feels thick—like we both know what needs to be said, but neither of us knows where to start.

He lets out a slow breath, like he's been holding it in for years. Then he turns to face me, really face me.

"Annabelle," he says, voice lower than usual, "I've been thinking. About what you said. About Marcus. About all of it."

I brace myself, heart skipping a little. "And?"

He stares down at his hands for a second, the way he always does when he's working through something big. "I didn't mean to push you away. I guess somewhere along the line, protecting you started to feel more important than understanding you."

My throat tightens. It's not much. But it's honest.

"I know," I say. "You were trying to keep me safe. You always have. But, Dad... Marcus isn't who you think he is. Not anymore."

He doesn't argue. Doesn't shut down. Just nods a little, like he's still figuring it out.

"Maybe I was wrong about him," he says. "I still don't like how things ended back then, but... yesterday? I heard about the party from your friends, about how happy you seemed to be with him—they said they haven't seen you that alive in a long time." He glances at me. "It's hard to argue with how happy you looked. I saw a photo."

A flicker of hope rises in my chest even though it's kind of weird to think about how my friends conspired behind my back. *They had good intentions*, I try to convince myself.

My hope is shaky, but it's real.

"So... you're okay with us?" I ask, trying not to sound too eager.

He shrugs, but not like he's brushing it off—more like he's being honest. "I'm not saying I'm thrilled. But I'm also not blind. You're stronger now. More sure of yourself. That's not something I should be standing in the way of. And if Marcus is part of that... then no, I won't fight you on it."

I swallow hard, feeling something soft and heavy loosen in my chest. "Thank you. Really."

He looks at me with that quiet dad expression he saves for big moments—the ones he doesn't quite know how to word. "Just promise me something?"

"Anything."

"Be careful with your heart. And if he ever forgets how lucky he is, well..." He taps his boot against the porch rail. "I still have that shotgun in the shed."

A laugh bubbles out of me before I can stop it. "You and your dramatic threats."

"Dramatic?" He smirks. "I thought that was pretty restrained."

I shake my head, smiling. For once, it feels easy. Like maybe we're not on opposite sides anymore.

He leans over and wraps an arm around me. Not tight. Not forced. Just steady. Familiar. The kind of hug that says I've still got you, even if I don't always understand you.

"I love you, kid," he murmurs. "All I've ever wanted was for you to be happy."

"I know," I whisper, my voice catching. "And I love you too, Dad. I think... I really think I'm finding that happiness now."

He squeezes my shoulder, then lets go, his gaze returning to the yard.

We sit there a while, not saying much. Just listening to

the wind rustle through the trees, letting the quiet do its own kind of healing.

And for the first time in a long time, I don't feel pulled between two pieces of my life.

I just feel whole.

~

It's just past dusk when I hear the crunch of gravel in the driveway.

Marcus.

I'd asked him to come by after Dad and I talked—needed time to let everything settle before I saw him again. But now that he's here, just the sight of him walking toward me under the porch light makes something flutter in my chest.

"Hey," he says, voice soft, almost careful. "How'd it go?"

I smile before I can even answer, the weight of the last hour still lifting off my shoulders. "Better than I thought it would. He… he gave us his blessing."

Marcus stops in his tracks, blinking. "Wait. Seriously?"

"Yeah," I nod. "Reluctant? Definitely. But real. He meant it."

Marcus lets out a long breath, like he's been holding it for weeks. His shoulders finally relax. "That's… wow. I didn't see that coming."

I grin, stepping toward him. "Right? Who knew miracles actually happen in Fairhope?"

He laughs, that easy sound that always makes me feel a little more grounded. Then he reaches for my hands—warm, steady—and just like that, everything feels real.

"Annabelle," he says, voice lower now, "that means everything."

"I know," I say, lacing my fingers through his. "It's like

—for the first time—it's not just us trying to swim against the current. We finally get to *be*."

Marcus watches me closely, his thumb moving slowly across the back of my hand. "No more hiding. No more walking on eggshells."

"Nope," I smile. "We get to make our own rules now. Start over."

His hands come up to cup my face, gentle and sure. His touch is familiar, but it feels new all at once—like a promise. "There's nothing I want more than that."

My heart stumbles in my chest, but in the best way. "Me too."

He leans in, forehead resting against mine, and we both just breathe for a second. The air between us is full of everything we've been through, all the broken pieces we've finally put back in place.

"From now on," he murmurs, "every memory counts. The good, the messy... all of it."

"Ours," I whisper.

And when he kisses me, it's slow. No pressure. Just warmth and understanding and something that feels a lot like coming home.

When he pulls back, his hand lingers on my cheek, and there's a light in his eyes I haven't seen since we were kids —something hopeful and open.

"So," he says with a small smile, "what now?"

I bite my lip, trying not to grin too much. "I might have a plan."

He raises an eyebrow. "A plan, huh?"

"Mm-hmm." I lean in a little, teasing. "Something that makes this new beginning really stick."

"Oh yeah?" His smile turns curious. "You gonna tell me what it is?"

"Not yet," I say, squeezing his hand. "But it involves us.

Somewhere quiet. Just the two of us. A place where we can start this new chapter for real."

He laughs softly, shaking his head. "You're killing me, you know that?"

"But you're still all in?" I ask.

He doesn't hesitate. "Every part of me."

My breath catches a little. I squeeze his hand again, firmer this time. "Good. Because this time, Marcus Gray, we're not letting the past call the shots. We get to write the ending."

His eyes light up, and for the first time in forever, the weight in my chest is just... gone.

"That sounds perfect," he says.

And the thing is? It *does*.

For the first time since the accident, since I lost my footing—since I lost *him*—I feel like I'm standing on solid ground again.

And this time, I'm not standing alone.

We're finally home.

BUILDING EXPECTATIONS

Marcus

*W*e're in my rented cabin today, and everything feels new. Nothing much has changed, yet everything has somehow.

The early morning sun spills through the kitchen window, lighting everything up in that soft golden way that makes even chaos look beautiful.

Annabelle and I are surrounded by open notebooks, pages of sketches, and a ridiculous amount of colored markers spread out across the kitchen table. It looks like an art supply store exploded in here. And I wouldn't change a thing.

She's fully in the zone—cheeks pink, hair in that messy knot she does when she's thinking hard, eyes locked on the paper in front of her like the future's hidden between the lines.

Watching her like this—focused, passionate, *happy*—it takes me back. Not just to when we were teenagers and the world was a little simpler, but to the version of her that's always been fiercely creative. Except now? There's something stronger behind her eyes. Something shaped by everything she's fought to come back from.

"Okay, Mr. Gray," she says, tapping her pen against her notebook with exaggerated seriousness. "Time to step up. I need help narrowing things down or my 'secret plan' is going to turn into, like, eighty different things I'll never finish."

I hold up my hands. "I'm ready. Hit me with the top contenders."

She flips through pages, skimming notes and colorful doodles until she pauses at one. "Alright, first: a community art studio. A space where kids—heck, anyone—can come and just make stuff. Second: remember that local art magazine idea I used to talk about? Bringing that back, but for real this time. And third…" She pauses, glancing at me, "teaching art classes at the community center."

I nod, genuinely impressed. "You'd kill it at all three. But I gotta say, the magazine idea? I remember you sketching mock covers way back when. You were so serious about it."

Her eyebrows rise. "Wait—*you* remember that?"

I grin. "Of course I do. We were out at the lake one afternoon, roasting in the sun. You were sketching logo ideas, and I was trying not to turn into a lobster."

Annabelle's face lights up. "Oh my God, yes! You were all dramatic about your shoulders burning, and I told you to stop being a baby."

"You teased me for *weeks*."

"You *deserved* it." She laughs, nudging me with her elbow.

The sound of her laughter does something to me. It's this weird combination of comfort and thrill—like I just stepped back into a memory I didn't know I missed.

I nudge her right back. "We made a good team, you know. Still do."

Her smile softens, eyes drifting back down to her notes. "It feels good, remembering stuff like that. Like I'm putting myself back together one sketch at a time."

"You didn't lose who you were," I say, leaning over to brush her hand gently. "She was just... taking a break."

She looks up at me, and there's this quiet kind of glow in her eyes—the kind that says *thank you* without needing the words. "You know, it helps having someone around who remembers the stuff I don't."

I smile. "Guess I'm good for more than just being dramatic about sunburn."

She snorts. "Barely."

I lean back in my chair, stretching. "So, back to business. If we're doing this magazine thing, we're gonna need a name."

She taps her pen against her lip, thinking. "Ugh, names are the hardest."

"What about something simple?" I offer. "Like... *Fairhope Sketchbook*."

She stops. Blinks. Then smiles. "That's actually kind of perfect. Feels personal. Local. Artsy but not pretentious."

I point at her with mock pride. "Just like you."

"Oh my God," she groans, rolling her eyes. "You're *impossible*."

"And yet," I smirk, "you still love me."

She tilts her head, lips curling into that playful smile I can never resist. "Yeah, maybe a little."

I grin and lean over, stealing a quick kiss on her cheek. "I'll take it."

She laughs again, scribbling *Fairhope Sketchbook* in big, looping letters across the page.

And in that moment—sitting here in a kitchen full of color, with her beside me and our dreams sprawled out between us—I know we're not just rewriting our past.

We're building something brand new.

Together.

~

By the time afternoon rolls around, our stack of sketches and scribbled notes has turned into something real—something that actually looks like a plan.

We're sitting on the front steps of Annabelle's porch, sipping coffee, sun warm on our shoulders. The quiet stretches around us like a soft blanket, peaceful and earned.

She leans against me, her shoulder resting lightly against mine. "Do you think we're dreaming too big?" she asks, voice low. "Like… is this really something we can pull off? Starting fresh. Actually chasing dreams."

I glance over, the way her brow creases just a little. She's nervous, yeah, but hopeful too. I slip my arm around her and pull her in closer.

"I do," I say. "I think it's real, and I think it's worth it. You're talented, you've got the drive—and Fairhope needs someone like you. I'll be here for all of it."

She lets out a long breath, leaning into me more. "It just feels scary, you know? Dreams are safe when they're in your head. But putting them out there? That makes them fragile. Like they could crack."

I nod. "You're right. But maybe the key is starting with something you *can* handle. Monthly issues instead of weekly. Partnering with local shops instead of doing it all alone. Keep it simple until it grows."

She looks up at me, smiling crookedly. "Wow. Since when did *you* become the practical one?"

I shrug and sip my coffee. "Spending time with you has that effect. I've clearly leveled up."

Annabelle laughs and nudges me with her elbow. "Smooth."

"Effective, though," I grin.

We sit like that for a while, taking it in. The quiet. The comfort. The idea that we're actually building something here—not just in theory, but together.

After a bit, she speaks again. "Hey… have you thought about what you want? Like, long-term? Beyond just being here with me?"

Her voice is gentle, but it hits something inside me. I hesitate, fingers tightening around my coffee cup.

"To be honest," I say, "not really. Coming back here was all about facing the stuff I ran from—and about being here for you. But watching you chase your dreams like this? It's starting to make me wonder what mine are."

She turns toward me, soft understanding in her eyes. "Well... whatever you figure out, I hope I'm in it."

My heart does this slow, steady swell. "You are. No matter what comes next—you're part of it."

She smiles and leans her head against my shoulder. "Good. This? Right here? Feels exactly like where I want to be."

Later that night, we're cleaning up dishes after dinner, bumping into each other in that easy rhythm couples fall into. She hums while rinsing a plate. I dry, mostly just watching her.

It's funny how couple-y we have become within this short amount of time. I can imagine this becoming my life, and it excites me. I smile sheepishly at myself and shake my head. *You're letting your thoughts run wild again, Marcus.*

Then my phone buzzes across the counter.

I glance at the screen, and my stomach tightens instantly.

It's a number I haven't seen in months.

Annabelle catches the shift in my expression. "You okay?"

I stare at the screen a second longer, then pick up. "Hello?"

A voice I didn't expect rumbles through the line. "Marcus, it's Coach Reynolds. How you been, son?"

I blink. "Coach? Wow, hey. Uh—doing alright. What's up?"

He doesn't waste time. "Heard you were back in Fairhope. Helping out at the sports center. I've got a buddy coaching at a college a few hours from here—he needs someone to step in and run the quarterback program. You came to mind right away."

I grip the counter a little tighter. "That's... unexpected."

"I know it's short notice," he says. "But it's a real opportunity. Something you could build on. I wouldn't have called if I didn't think you were ready."

I rub a hand down my face. "I appreciate that, Coach. I do. But I've got a lot to think about."

"Of course. Just don't toss it aside. Think it over. Sometimes second chances show up when you least expect them."

We hang up a few minutes later. I stare at the phone in my hand, trying to wrap my head around what just happened.

Annabelle's standing across from me, drying her hands on a dish towel. "What was that?"

I look up at her, feeling like the air just got a little heavier. "It was my old coach. He offered me a job. Quarterback coach. College team. A few hours from here."

Her expression changes—confused, a little shaken—but she nods. "Oh. Wow."

I step toward her quickly. "I'm not jumping at it,

Annabelle. I'm not leaving. I just… it caught me off guard."

She's quiet for a second. Then: "You deserve something for yourself, too, Marcus. You've given up a lot. If this is something you want, I don't want to be the reason you say no."

I reach for her hands. "You're not a reason to say no. You're *the* reason I came back in the first place. Whatever I decide, it's not just about me anymore. It's about *us*."

Her grip tightens slightly. She nods, voice soft. "Just promise me… we'll talk about it. Really talk. No bottling it up. No disappearing."

I nod. "Promise. Together, remember?"

"Together," she repeats, but there's a flicker of something behind her eyes—doubt, fear, maybe both. I feel it too, humming low in my chest.

Because as much as I want to stay rooted here with her, part of me is still wondering if this is *the* shot I thought I'd never get again.

Now I just have to figure out how to chase the future without letting go of the best thing I've found.

Her.

DECISIONS AND DESTINIES

Annabelle

I can't stop replaying the look in Marcus's eyes when he told me about the coaching offer. He tried to sound calm, reassuring, even optimistic. But beneath the confident front, I saw that same flicker of uncertainty that mirrors my own fears.

I want to be happy for him—really, I do—but a quiet dread settles in my stomach every time I think about the possibility of him leaving again.

I lean back in my chair, staring at the half-finished sketches of the *Fairhope Sketchbook* logo scattered across my desk. The dreams we started building feel shakier today, like carefully stacked cards vulnerable to the slightest breeze.

My eyes drift closed, and suddenly memories swirl, pulling me gently backward through time. Images flash softly in my mind—a younger Marcus, duffel bag slung over his shoulder, standing at the edge of my porch. He had that same hesitant look in his eyes then, one part excitement and two parts regret.

"This is my only way forward," he had said softly, eyes pleading with me to understand. *"I can't stay here, Annabelle."*

I remember how tightly I'd wanted to hug him, my heart splintering quietly, but I didn't. I smiled bravely, telling him it was fine, that I'd be okay. I knew he was leaving me behind, not even caring about how I'd feel. He was so focused on getting away... and I couldn't really blame him.

But after he drove away, the tears wouldn't stop falling, and I realized just how deeply I'd loved him.

It hits me suddenly—this is exactly what I've feared all along. Marcus leaving again, chasing a dream far away, leaving me behind.

I blink back the memory, heart aching softly. But it's different this time, isn't it? We're older, stronger. Marcus isn't running away now; he's chasing something he's earned. And he's not leaving me—he's sharing this choice with me. Yet the old wound throbs quietly, a gentle warning that loving Marcus will always mean embracing uncertainty.

I take a deep breath, wiping a tear from my cheek, determined not to let fear guide me this time.

Marcus shows up just as the sky starts melting into shades of pink and orange. I might sound like a dreamer, but I feel like sunsets make you believe in second chances. The beautiful hues always promise a better night and a hopeful tomorrow.

He steps into the room quietly, eyes soft, searching, as if he already knows I've been thinking too much.

He doesn't say anything right away—just sits beside me on the edge of the bed and reaches for my hand. His fingers slide into mine, warm and steady.

"You alright?" he asks, voice low, his eyes not letting go of mine.

I give him a small smile—one of those that looks braver than it feels—and squeeze his hand. "Trying to be," I say. "Marcus, this offer… it's amazing. You deserve it."

He sighs, nodding, like he's been waiting for me to say that, even if it's not what he wanted to hear. "I know it stirs up some stuff."

"It does." My voice cracks just a little. "I remember what it felt like the first time. Watching you leave. Waiting for a call that never came. I was heartbroken, and now it feels like I'm standing in that same doorway again, hoping it won't slam shut."

His brow tightens, guilt flashing across his face. "Annabelle, I hate that I put you through that. If I could undo any of it, I would."

"I know you didn't mean to," I say, quieter now. "And I'm not angry. But hearing about this coaching job… it hit me. We're closer now than we've ever been, and suddenly it feels like I could lose you again."

Marcus shifts, turning fully toward me, his hand still wrapped around mine. "That's exactly why this time is different. I'm not running. Not from you. Not from us. Yeah, the job's a big deal, but compared to what we have? It's nothing."

I study his face, my heart softening at how certain he looks.

"So… does that mean you're not taking it?" I ask, not really sure if I want the answer or if I'm just bracing for it.

He shakes his head slowly. "I haven't decided. Not yet. But whatever happens, it won't be *my* decision alone. I want us to figure it out together. If I take it, we'll make it work. Long-distance, road trips, smoke signals—whatever it takes. I'm not losing you again."

His words settle something in me. They don't erase the fear, but they quiet it.

"We've both grown a lot," I say. "I'm not the girl who needed protecting anymore. And you... you've become someone who thinks things through. Someone I trust."

He smiles a little, leaning forward until our foreheads touch, his hand trailing up to cradle my jaw. "That means more than you know."

I let the moment hang between us for a breath before whispering, "But what do *you* want, Marcus? Take me out of it. If nobody else had a say, what would your gut tell you?"

He pulls back slightly, exhaling through his nose. "For the longest time, football was everything. It was all I had, all I chased. But since being back... since *you*... I've realized I want more than a title or a paycheck. I want to build something that matters. I want a life with roots. And I want it with you."

My chest tightens, not from anxiety this time, but from something warm and full. "That's what I want too. But I need you to know—you're allowed to have dreams, Marcus. You don't need to give them up for me."

He cups my cheek again, gently this time. "Being with you doesn't feel like giving anything up. It feels like I finally *found* what I was always missing."

I close my eyes for a second, soaking in his touch, the truth of it.

"So," I say, sitting back in my chair, a smile creeping in, "how do you feel about doing something a little spontaneous?"

Marcus raises a brow, amused. "That smile makes me nervous. What are you scheming?"

"A celebration," I say, grinning now. "Right now. No overthinking, no planning. Just us... and maybe a few people we love. Something to mark the fact that we're still here, still choosing each other."

He looks intrigued. "Okay… I'm listening."

I lean in a little. "How about a bonfire? The old lake spot. You, me, maybe Ethan, Abby. A small night to just *be*. Close one chapter, open the next."

His smile widens, his whole expression lighting up. "You really want to do that *tonight*?"

"Why not?" I shrug. "We've waited long enough to live fully. Let's stop waiting for perfect timing and just make it count."

Marcus laughs, that low, warm sound I love. "Annabelle Dawson, when did you get so bold?"

"Probably around the time you started quoting life advice back to me."

He chuckles, then lifts my hand and presses a kiss to my knuckles. "I love this version of you. The one who charges ahead with a plan and drags me with her."

"Good," I say, playful but sure. "Because she's not going anywhere."

He grins, his voice soft but solid. "Then yeah—let's do it. Bonfire tonight. No fear. No pressure. Just us and the people who matter."

I nod, a swell of excitement rising in my heart. "Perfect. Let's make it one to remember."

Marcus leans in, brushing a kiss against my forehead. "Every moment with you already is."

And even though the coaching lurks in the background like a quiet drumbeat, I let it fade for now. Because tonight isn't about what we might lose.

Tonight is about everything we've already found.

And we've come too far to let fear steal this moment.

Not tonight.

CELEBRATION OF LOVE

Marcus

I never thought I'd be the guy who plans a spontaneous proposal at a bonfire. Then again, I never thought I'd willingly watch a reality dating show with Ethan, yet here we are. Life's weird like that.

I grip the little velvet box in my jacket pocket, my pulse racing. Tonight's supposed to be casual—marshmallows, s'mores, and embarrassing stories—but as soon as Annabelle suggested this celebration, I knew I wanted to make it more.

It might seem rushed, but honestly, when you know, you just know. Plus, Ethan said, "If you chicken out now, I'll propose to Annabelle myself." The thought alone is terrifying enough to push me forward.

The lake sparkles under the setting sun, a perfect back-drop for a memory I hope Annabelle and I cherish forever. Our friends are scattered around, laughter carrying through the cool evening air. Ethan's busy building a fire, Abby's setting up chairs with Sarah, and Charlie is enthusi-astically (and very badly) singing along to whatever playlist he's chosen—probably titled *Greatest Hits No One Actually Wants to Hear.*

Annabelle is chatting with Abby, smiling wider than I've seen in ages. Seeing her this happy settles something in my chest, confirming that I'm making the right choice. Or at least, a crazy choice I won't regret.

Ethan walks over, smacking my shoulder. "Dude, you're sweating buckets. Chill out. She'll say yes."

I glare half-heartedly. "Thanks for that vote of confidence. And I'm not sweating—it's warm."

"It's sixty degrees," he deadpans. "And you look like you just sprinted here."

"Maybe I'm nervous she'll laugh and say no," I mutter, glancing at Annabelle nervously. She catches my eye and gives me a wink, which makes my stomach flip.

"Laugh? Yeah, probably. Say no? Doubtful," Ethan grins. "But hey, if she does, I'll buy you ice cream. Deal?"

"You're the worst friend ever," I groan, shoving him lightly.

He chuckles, dodging back. "Aw, Marcus, I love you too. Now go make sure Charlie doesn't set himself on fire. Again."

I head toward Charlie, who's currently holding marshmallows way too close to a match. "Charlie, man, you need help?"

He glances up sheepishly. "Fire's hard, Marcus."

"Maybe for you," I laugh, taking over. "How about you just handle the music?"

"You doubt my fire-starting skills, but trust my music taste?" he asks, raising an eyebrow.

"Oh, I doubt both. But music won't burn down the dock," I joke, lighting the small pyramid of kindling. The flame catches quickly, crackling softly.

Annabelle rolls over, settling next to me. "You look suspiciously stressed for a bonfire."

I smile sheepishly. "Oh, you know, just worried about Charlie accidentally torching something valuable."

She laughs, leaning closer. "As long as it's not your jacket. I like how you look in it."

My heartbeat picks up again as I squeeze her hand, the ring pressing gently against my fingertips from inside my pocket. She has no idea how significant tonight's about to become.

"Trust me, I'll protect the jacket at all costs," I promise.

She smirks playfully, eyes twinkling. "Good. But just so you know, it's what's under the jacket that counts."

I nearly choke, face heating instantly. Tonight, Annabelle's laughter, our friends' teasing, the crackling fire —everything is exactly how I envisioned our life could be: perfectly imperfect.

Now, I just need to find the right moment to make tonight a night we never forget.

By the time night folds completely over Fairhope, the sky's lit up with stars that look like someone strung fairy lights across the heavens just for us. The fire crackles nearby, sending orange sparks into the cool air, and our little group —me, Annabelle, and the ride-or-dies—sits scattered around it, full from dinner, full of stories, full of something we haven't all felt together in a while: peace.

Annabelle leans against me, her arm brushing mine, her head close enough I can feel her laugh when Ethan launches into one of his infamous over-the-top tales.

"So then," he says, gesturing dramatically with a slightly burnt marshmallow, "Marcus, in his infinite genius, decides *he's* going to rescue the football from Principal Hank's roof. Only he ends up getting stuck himself. The fire department was involved. I kid you not."

Laughter explodes around the fire. Even I crack a smile, though I groan a little for show.

"It wasn't that bad," I mumble, half-laughing.

"Oh, it was *absolutely* that bad," Charlie says, his grin wide. "Hank had to call the ladder truck. You were a full-on rooftop damsel in distress."

"Legend," Ethan says with mock solemnity. "We salute you."

Beside me, Annabelle's shoulders shake with laughter. "I still think you're pretty heroic," she says, nudging me. "Even if your climbing skills are questionable."

I shoot her a mock glare. "Thanks for the moral support."

She beams. "Anytime."

Her eyes lock with mine, and just for a second, everything else fades—the jokes, the chatter, even the fire. It's just her and me, starlight dancing across her face, her expression soft and full of something deeper than laughter.

"Um, hello?" Abby teases, clearing her throat. "Some of us are still here."

Annabelle blushes and ducks her head, laughing. "Sorry, got distracted."

Sarah smirks, roasting another marshmallow. "We'll allow it. Barely. You two are disgustingly cute."

Charlie grins. "Like, Hallmark-movie cute. Needs a soundtrack and a snowstorm."

Annabelle rolls her eyes. "You're all impossible."

Ethan raises his burnt marshmallow like a toast. "But we're *your* impossible. And Marcus is our fearless—if occasionally roof-stuck—leader."

"I'm never living that down, am I?" I mutter.

Ethan claps my shoulder. "Not in this lifetime."

Before he can launch into another story, I cut him off. "Save some of that for the wedding."

Everyone laughs. They think I'm joking. That's fine. For now.

Across the fire, Annabelle squeezes my hand. "This is perfect, Marcus. I couldn't ask for more."

I glance at her, then toward the stars, then back again. The ring in my pocket feels heavier now. Not in a bad way —just... important.

"Neither could I," I say.

She studies me for a beat, her expression turning soft. "You think it'll always feel like this?"

"Like what?"

"Like home," she murmurs. "Safe. Happy. Like it's okay to hope again."

I lean in a little closer. "That's what we're building, Belle. And it's not just this place. It's us."

She smiles, and I swear it warms something deep in my chest. "You're getting dangerously romantic," she whispers.

"I'll try not to ruin my tough-guy image," I say, smirking.

"Oh, please," she says with a laugh. "That ship sailed when you cried during that dog movie."

"One time," I mutter. "And the dog *died*. That's emotional warfare."

She laughs again, and I don't care that everyone's watching. I could live inside her laugh forever.

Eventually, one by one, our friends start packing up. Ethan stretches dramatically. "Alright, I think this third wheel's about to roll."

Charlie claps my shoulder on his way out. "No more roof rescues, okay?"

"No promises."

Abby leans in and whispers to Annabelle loud enough for me to hear, "Don't keep him up too late. He might decide to climb something again."

Annabelle rolls her eyes, giggling. "Goodnight, guys."

And just like that, it's quiet. Just me, Annabelle, and the glow of dying embers.

She sighs, content. "Tonight was everything."

I nod, heart thumping a little harder. "There's something else," I say quietly. "Something I've been holding onto."

She looks up. "Yeah?"

"Come take a walk with me?"

She gives me that curious little smile. "Okay."

I help her toward the dock, the moon spilling silver light across the water. The lake is still, like it's holding its breath.

"You're acting suspicious," she says as we reach the end.

I turn toward her, take both her hands in mine. Her fingers are cool from the night air, and her eyes are wide, waiting.

"Annabelle," I start, voice steady even as my chest tightens, "this whole night—it wasn't just about celebrating the past. It was about what's next. And I've realized something. I don't want next to happen without you."

She stares at me, breath catching.

"I want it all," I continue. "The easy days, the hard ones, the quiet mornings, the messy fights, and everything in between. I want it with *you*. Every bit of it."

Her eyes start to shimmer, but she doesn't say anything yet.

I smile nervously. "You've made me braver, Belle. Kinder. More me than I've ever been. And loving you... it's the best decision I've ever made."

I reach into my pocket and pull out the ring. Her hand flies to her mouth, tears already forming.

"Is that—?"

"Yeah," I say, voice soft but sure. "Annabelle Dawson... will you marry me?"

THE PROMISE

Annabelle

*M*y breath catches in my throat as Marcus kneels in front of me, the moonlight making him look like a real-life Prince Charming. The diamond in the little velvet box catches the glow, sure—but it's not the ring that makes my heart lurch.

It's *him*.

That look in his eyes—open, vulnerable, full of love. Like he's holding his breath right along with me.

My heart feels like it's going to burst. I'm full to the brim with everything—shock, joy, disbelief, the kind of happiness that fills every corner of your chest until it's all you can feel.

"Marcus…" I whisper, voice barely holding steady. "Are you really sure?"

He laughs, quiet and warm, like I just asked the most ridiculous question in the world. "Annabelle, I've never been more sure of anything. I love you. Always have. And I want my life to be about loving you—and making you ridiculously happy."

His words wash over me like sunlight. Every fear, every what-if, every part of me that ever wondered if this kind of love could really last—it all falls quiet.

Tears prick my eyes, but I don't try to stop them. I *want* to feel this. I *want* to remember what it's like to say yes with your whole heart.

"Yes," I breathe, the answer falling out of me like it's always been waiting. "Yes, Marcus. Absolutely, yes."

His smile spreads so wide I almost forget how to breathe. He slides the ring onto my finger, and it fits like it was made for me—like it always belonged there.

Like *he* always belonged with me.

Marcus rises slowly, hands cupping my face so gently it nearly undoes me all over again. His eyes meet mine, steady and full of something deeper than words—something safe. Real. Fierce.

"You just made me the luckiest man alive," he says, voice low.

"And you made me the happiest," I whisper, leaning into his hands. "I still can't believe we're here."

"Me neither," he says, thumb brushing my cheek. "But I'm so damn grateful we are."

I laugh, breathless and full of something bigger than I can name. "I love you, Marcus."

His smile softens. "I love you too. And I promise, I'll never stop."

And then he kisses me—slow and sure, like it's the only thing he's certain of in this world. This is a kiss that doesn't need fireworks or fanfare because it's built on something better—something solid.

It's a kiss that says *home*.

The stars glitter above us. The lake whispers at our feet. And everything, for once, feels exactly right.

When we finally pull apart, I can't stop smiling. My heart feels like it's glowing.

"Marcus Gray," I say, still catching my breath, "you just made my dreams come true."

He chuckles, forehead resting lightly against mine. "Good. Because I plan on doing that again tomorrow. And the next day. And every day after that."

And I believe him.

Because this isn't a dream anymore.

This is *us*—stronger, braver, and finally whole.

Marcus wraps his arms around me, pulling me in tight against his chest. I melt into him, breathing him in—the steady rhythm of his heart, the strength of his arms, the warmth that settles over me like a blanket.

We stand there for a while, no words, just the fire crackling behind us and the sound of the lake lapping gently against the dock. It's one of those quiet miracles—simple, soft, but it feels like everything.

Finally, his voice breaks the silence, low and close to my ear. "Did I surprise you?"

I laugh against his chest, my hand slipping up to rest over his heart. "Completely. But it feels... right. Like this was always where we were supposed to end up."

He kisses my forehead, slow and warm. "I wanted tonight to be something you'd never forget."

"You pulled that off," I murmur, tipping my head to look at him. "I still feel like I'm floating."

His eyes crinkle with a soft smile. "Hopefully not because of nerves."

"No," I say, grinning. "Because of you."

We stand like that a moment longer, and then I hear him chuckle.

"What?"

"I was just thinking," he says, eyes full of affection, "hopefully our future has fewer rooftop rescues."

I giggle, nudging his ribs gently. "Speak for yourself. Those stories are gold."

He shakes his head, laughing. "Okay, fair. But I'm aiming for less fire department drama and more… mornings on the porch. Dinners with friends. Lazy weekends. You, me, a quiet kind of forever."

Something about the way he says it—simple, sincere—makes my heart flutter.

"You really want that?" I ask, voice quieter now. "A life here. With me. Something small and real?"

Marcus doesn't hesitate. "Annabelle, I'd follow you anywhere. But if life keeps us in Fairhope, then that's not settling—that's exactly where I want to be. It doesn't have to be flashy. Just honest. Just ours."

My throat tightens. Tears sting again, soft and grateful this time.

"You have no idea how much that means to me."

He lifts a hand, brushing a strand of hair behind my ear. "I think I have a pretty good idea."

He leans in and kisses me again—slow, unhurried, like he's trying to memorize the feel of this moment. I kiss him back, smiling against his lips, wrapped in something so full and steady it makes everything before feel like a prelude.

I rest my head against his shoulder, eyes drifting to the ring glinting on my finger. It's more than just a ring—it's a symbol of everything we've rebuilt. Trust. Growth. Love that stayed quiet until it was strong enough to be spoken aloud.

"We're really getting married," I whisper, still a little breathless.

Marcus lets out a small laugh. "Honestly? Part of me still thinks this is a dream."

I grin and give his arm a quick pinch.

"Ow!" he says with mock offense, rubbing the spot. "Okay, definitely real."

"Good," I whisper, kissing his cheek. "Because I don't ever want to wake up from this."

His arms tighten around me. "Even when things get messy again—because they will—I promise I'll be right here. I'll remind you every single day how real this is. How real we are."

I nod, my voice thick. "That's a promise I'll hold you to."

The sound of gravel crunching behind us pulls me from his arms. I turn, surprised, and feel my breath hitch.

"Dad?"

He steps into the moonlight, fiddling with the buttons on his coat, eyes soft and tired—but kind.

"I didn't mean to interrupt," he says. "Marcus invited me. Thought I should be here tonight."

I glance back at Marcus, caught off guard. "You... you planned this?"

He nods, a little sheepish. "Felt important. I talked to him earlier. I wanted him to know where I stand—and I wanted you to have your dad here. For this."

I turn back to my father, heart hammering in my chest, not from fear but something gentler. Hope.

Dad walks closer, his gaze moving between the two of us. "I've watched you change, Annabelle. These past few weeks... I've seen you come back to yourself. You're stronger. Happier. You're you again. And I think I have Marcus to thank for that."

Marcus shifts awkwardly. "She's always had that strength. I just got lucky enough to witness it."

Dad gives him a long look. Then he nods slowly. "I was wrong about you, Marcus. I held on too tightly to the past. I let fear guide me. But tonight, seeing you two like this? I get it now."

He turns fully to me, voice quiet. "You have my blessing, Annabelle. Fully. No hesitation."

Tears break free again, this time with nothing but joy behind them. "Dad… thank you."

He squeezes my hands. "You deserve this, sweetheart. And now I can see it clearly—he's your happiness."

I step back toward Marcus, heart full. "You didn't have to do that," I whisper.

"Yeah," he says, brushing a tear off my cheek, "but I wanted to."

Dad gives Marcus a nod of respect and claps his shoulder. "Take care of her."

Marcus meets his gaze, steady and sure. "Always."

Dad steps back into the shadows, heading home. I watch him disappear, then turn to Marcus with tears still in my eyes.

"You really thought of everything."

"I tried," he says with a soft smile. "I wanted tonight to feel like the start of something real."

"It is," I whisper. "You didn't just propose—you gave me back something I thought I lost. Family. Home."

Marcus pulls me into him again, resting his chin gently on top of my head. "You gave me something too. A second chance. I won't waste it."

I close my eyes and breathe him in. "Marcus?"

"Yeah?"

"This is just the beginning," I whisper.

He lifts my chin so I'm looking straight into his eyes. "Then let's make it one hell of a beginning."

I nod, smiling as he kisses me again—beneath the stars, beside the lake, with the firelight fading and a brand-new chapter rising right in front of us.

NEW HORIZONS

Marcus

*T*he next few days are... well, wild. In the best small-town way.

Fairhope feels like it just discovered it's been living inside a soap opera—except instead of scandal or betrayal, it's all "Did you hear? Marcus and Annabelle are engaged!"

And apparently, that's headline-worthy around here.

Everywhere we go, people stop us. Smiles. Hugs. "About times." A few happy tears. A lot of pie.

Mrs. Lewis at the bakery has decided we're her new charity project—she's been slipping us extra cinnamon rolls every morning like she's trying to fatten us up for winter. Charlie? He keeps patting me on the back like I just survived something major. And Ethan's taken it upon himself to deliver a running commentary on the death of my singlehood.

"So, this is it, huh?" he says yesterday while handing me a soda. "No more last-minute road trips. No more 2 a.m. video game tournaments. I'm losing you to domestic bliss."

"You'll survive," I told him.

"Barely," he muttered, sipping dramatically.

This morning, though, it's just me and Annabelle. We're camped out on her front porch, surrounded by open magazines, old sketchbooks, sticky notes, and coffee cups we keep forgetting to refill. Annabelle is in full creative mode, and honestly? It's kind of mesmerizing.

She flips through a notepad, twirling a pencil between her fingers like it's part of a ritual. "Okay, hear me out," she says. "What if we start with a quarterly release? Not too overwhelming, but still consistent enough to build interest."

I sip my coffee and nod. "Makes sense. And each issue could spotlight a local artist or business. Give the town something to rally around."

Her eyes light up. "Yes! It should feel like Fairhope. Real people. Real stories."

I grin. "Good. Everyone here loves seeing themselves in print—especially if there's a chance their cousin's best friend's dog makes the cut."

She laughs, leaning against me. "Ethan already offered to be our first subscriber."

"He probably thinks it gets him into some exclusive club."

"As long as he doesn't ask for a 'Best Friend Discount.'"

I raise a brow. "He already did. I told him it would double his rate."

Annabelle giggles, then rests her head gently on my shoulder. I feel her smile before I see it. "You know," she murmurs, "I really love this."

I glance at her, brushing a strand of hair away from her cheek. "The porch or the stack of notebooks?"

She looks up, eyes warm. "This. All of it. Planning

something real together. Building something that feels like ours."

I squeeze her hand. "Yeah. I didn't think I'd get to have this. For a while, I thought maybe I didn't deserve it."

Her face softens. "Why?"

I look out across the yard for a second, watching a bird hop across the fence. "After my injury, everything just... collapsed. The future I'd banked on disappeared overnight. And I didn't know who I was without it. But coming back here—being with you—it reminded me that maybe I hadn't lost everything. I just lost track of what really mattered."

She shifts a little closer, her hand warm in mine. "Marcus, you gave that back to me too. My confidence. My voice. For a long time, I didn't think I'd ever feel like *me* again. But now I do."

I lean in and press a kiss to her forehead, slow and steady. "We've been through a lot. But together? I think we're kind of unstoppable."

Her smile turns playful. "Well, in that case, Mr. Gray, it's time we channeled that unstoppable energy into this magazine layout."

"Right. Focus. No more romantic monologuing."

She laughs. "One more compliment and I might let you off the hook for editing the intro column."

I shoot her a mock-serious look. "You drive a hard bargain."

"Deal?"

"Deal."

We dive back into our notes, side by side, pencils moving, ideas flying. We argue over fonts, vote on cover titles, debate whether or not we're allowed to include an entire page just for dogs (spoiler: we are). And through it all, it's easy.

We're building something, and not just the magazine. A rhythm. A partnership. A future.

And even though my coaching offer still sits quietly in the back of my mind, like a bookmark I haven't turned to yet, it doesn't feel heavy anymore. Because no matter where that choice takes me—or us—we've already decided what matters most.

We're in this together.

And that makes everything ahead a little less scary. And a whole lot more exciting.

～

Two days later, I surprise Annabelle with a date at Fairhope's newest hidden gem—**The Greenhouse Co.**, a little plant shop that just opened up on Main.

Not long ago, this place was just an empty storefront with boarded-up windows and peeling paint. Now? It smells like fresh soil and citrus leaves, and the windows glow like they're soaking in every drop of sunlight Fairhope has to offer. It's bright, peaceful, full of life—kind of like us lately.

I push Annabelle's wheelchair through the open door, and the bells above us jingle softly. The air is warm and earthy, the kind that smells like possibility. Plants of every shape and size are tucked into nooks and hanging from the ceiling—pothos trailing from hooks, sunflowers soaking in the light, tiny succulents sitting like quiet sentinels in terracotta pots.

"Marcus…" Annabelle breathes, her voice soft with wonder. "This place is *gorgeous*. When did this open?"

"Two weeks ago," I say, rolling us further in. "Ethan mentioned it, and I figured we could use a little green therapy."

She turns her head, eyes scanning the rows of leafy greens, flowering herbs, and shelves stacked with books and garden trinkets. "I can't believe this used to be that old appliance store."

I grin, steering us past a table filled with tiny air plants in seashells. "Yeah. All it took was someone seeing what it *could* be."

Annabelle glances up at me, her eyes warm. "That's very poetic, Marcus Gray."

I raise a brow, smirking. "I have my moments. Usually when I'm trying to impress a beautiful woman in a plant shop."

She laughs, eyes sparkling. "Careful. You keep that up, I'll start expecting poetry with my morning coffee."

"Tempting," I say, leaning down to press a kiss to her temple. "But I draw the line at rhyming before caffeine."

She rolls her eyes, still smiling, as we stop near a long wooden shelf stacked with colorful planters. Annabelle picks up a small clay pot shaped like a fox and holds it like it's the most precious thing she's ever seen.

"This place feels like a dream," she murmurs. "It's quiet, but full of life."

"Like us," I say, without even thinking.

She looks at me, her smile softening. "Yeah. Like us."

We make our way to the back, where a cozy nook has been set up with benches and hanging plants overhead. I help Annabelle transfer onto the bench beside me, wrapping an arm around her as she settles in. The light filters through the greenery like stained glass, warm and dappled.

After a few quiet moments, she turns to me, her voice calm but thoughtful. "So… how are you feeling about the coaching offer?"

I let out a slow breath, watching a dust mote drift through a sunbeam. "It's a lot. I mean, I'm excited. I didn't think I'd ever get another shot like that. But also… nervous. Because taking it means stepping back into that world again. Balancing everything."

She nods slowly, fingers brushing the edge of a nearby planter. "Do you think it's the *right* thing?"

I think about that. Really think.

"I think it *could* be. But being here, with you, helping you launch this magazine, this life… that feels just as right. I don't want to chase something so hard that I lose what we've built."

Annabelle leans into me, resting her head against my shoulder. "Maybe it's not about choosing between one or the other. Maybe it's just… figuring out how to do both."

I nod. "You'd be okay with the long-distance stuff? The time apart?"

She lifts her head slightly, her voice steady. "Marcus, we've already survived more than most couples go through in a lifetime. A few hours of highway won't break us."

I swallow the lump in my throat and squeeze her hand. "You'd really do that for me?"

She smiles, calm and sure. "We'd do it *together*. That's the whole point, right? This—*us*—only works when we both keep showing up. So if that means late-night calls and weekend visits for a while, I can handle that."

I nod, overwhelmed in the best way. "You've always been stronger than me."

"Don't sell yourself short," she says, brushing a hand across my jaw. "You came back when it counted. You stayed. And you're still here."

I kiss her gently, thankful that words can only go so far when your heart is full to bursting.

The breeze drifts in through the open doors, stirring the scent of rosemary and jasmine. Around us, the plants sway like they're part of something bigger—quiet, growing, alive.

"We should get something," she says suddenly, sitting up straighter.

"Like a plant?"

She nods, smiling. "Something we can keep together. Watch it grow. You know—symbolism."

I chuckle. "You mean responsibility?"

"That too."

We wander back toward the shelves, eventually landing on a small olive tree in a white ceramic pot. It's young, a little crooked, but already strong and rooted.

"This one," she says, gently touching one of its soft leaves. "It's a bit imperfect. But it's beautiful."

I grin, wrapping an arm around her waist. "Just like us."

And right there, in the middle of a plant shop in Fairhope, I know—we'll figure it out. Whatever path we take, whatever choices we make, we'll keep growing.

Together.

A few mornings later, we're sitting at a corner table in *The Nest*—Fairhope's new breakfast spot that smells like fresh-baked muffins and maple syrup. It's all cozy chairs, mismatched mugs, and sunlight streaming through wide windows. The place feels calm. Familiar.

Which is exactly why the sudden buzz of my phone nearly sends my coffee flying.

I glance down, and just like that, my stomach drops.

Coach Reynolds.

My pulse kicks up fast.

Annabelle looks up from her blueberry scone, brushing a crumb from her lip. "You okay?"

"It's Coach," I say, already feeling the nerves tighten in my chest. "This is probably *the* call."

She reaches across the table without hesitation, squeezing my hand. "Answer it. Whatever happens, we'll figure it out."

I nod, take a deep breath, and swipe to answer. "Hey, Coach. Morning."

"Marcus," he says, upbeat right out of the gate. "Hope you're ready for some good news."

I sit up straighter. "That definitely sounds promising."

"It is," he says, clearly excited. "My friend was impressed—really impressed. Not just with your football history, but with how involved you've been in Fairhope. They want to offer you the quarterback coach position. And—this is big—they also want you to head up a new community-outreach program for local kids who want to get into sports."

I blink, stunned. "Wait—both?"

"Both," he confirms. "They think you're the right person to build this thing. I do too. Marcus, this isn't just a job—it's impact. It's exactly where you're meant to be."

I glance at Annabelle across the table. She's watching me, eyes full of warmth, like she already knows. I nod slowly, still stunned. "Coach, I… wow. Thank you. I just need to think it through a little."

"Of course," he says. "Take your time. But I believe in this—and in you."

I hang up and set the phone down like it might start buzzing again.

Annabelle tilts her head. "Well?"

I let out a long breath. "They offered it. Officially. But it's more than I expected. Coaching *and* leading a new community program."

Her whole face lights up—pure joy. "Marcus, that's *amazing*! It's everything you care about. Coaching, kids, making a difference. All of it."

"Yeah," I say, smiling… but then the weight of it hits.

"It's just… a lot. More hours, more responsibility. And it's a few hours away, Annabelle. I'd be gone more. And I don't want that to mess with what we've just started building."

She leans in, placing her hand gently on my cheek. Her touch is steady, grounding.

"Marcus, this is your dream evolving. Of course it's going to stretch you. But you *can* do this. *We* can do this. I know we can."

I study her face—how sure she looks, even though I know she's just as scared of change as I am.

"You'd really be okay with it?" I ask quietly. "The late nights, the distance, the video calls instead of real ones?"

She nods, fingers brushing lightly along my jaw. "Of course I'd miss you. But I'd never hold you back from something this important. I *want* to see you grow. That's what love is, Marcus. We cheer for each other—even when the game gets hard."

That hits me in the chest, hard and warm.

"I don't deserve you," I whisper.

"You do," she says firmly, not even hesitating.

I lean across the table and kiss her—slow and grateful. The kind of kiss that says *thank you for believing in me* when I still have trouble believing in myself.

But when we pull apart and sit back in our seats, the quiet settles between us again—and this time it feels different. Heavier.

Because we both know what this means.

Our future just changed.

And yeah, we're smiling. Yeah, we're in love.

But we're also staring down something brand new—something bigger than either of us has faced before.

Neither of us says it out loud, but I know we're both thinking it:

Are we strong enough to hold all this together?

If this were me some months back, I would have doubted it. I would've doubted me. But I have changed. This a new, more confident me. A me who's so in love he knows he can do anything to protect his love.

EMBRACING CHANGE

Annabelle

The bright lights of the Fairhope Sports Center gleam overhead, and I squint a little as I push through my last set of leg extensions. My thighs burn in that oddly satisfying way—like my body's reminding me it's still capable of surprising me.

Samantha, my ever-patient physical therapist, gives me a grin from her clipboard. "That's the strongest set you've done all month, Annabelle. I think I owe you a smoothie."

I laugh, breathless but proud. "Make it a double shot of vanilla and I'll consider forgiving you for all those resistance bands."

"Deal," she winks, scribbling something down. "You're really getting your rhythm back."

I stretch my arms, already feeling the soreness sneak in, but I welcome it. A few months ago, this would've knocked the wind out of me. Now? It makes me feel alive. Capable. Whole.

The sound of sneakers squeaking on polished floors gives me a jump scare, but it's just a group of kids passing by, tossing a football between them. I glance out the wide glass window into the gymnasium.

For a second, I spot Marcus on the far end, clipboard in hand, laughing as he demonstrates a move to one of the teens. His voice echoes faintly, confident and warm, and my heart does that soft lurch it's been doing since the day he came back.

"Your fiancé's got a fan club," Samantha says teasingly, noticing my gaze.

"Oh, believe me, I'm aware," I smirk. "I've seen the way the PTA moms look at him."

She laughs. "Hey, it's small-town charm. But you're the only one he looks at like that."

I smile. "I know."

I lean back slightly in the chair, letting the last wave of muscle soreness fade. The ring on my finger catches a beam of afternoon sunlight and glints, drawing my eyes to it.

It still feels surreal sometimes—like all of this is someone else's story. A year ago, I couldn't even remember who Marcus was. I was still trying to recognize myself in the mirror. The girl I was then—quiet, tentative, stuck between who she used to be and who she was becoming— couldn't have imagined this moment.

But this? Sitting in a therapy room with trembling muscles and a full heart? This is mine. All of it.

Samantha gives me a soft pat on the shoulder. "Go cool down. You've earned it."

I nod and slowly wheel myself to the end of the room, where the wall-to-wall mirrors reflect the version of me I've fought hard to reclaim. I don't see the scared girl anymore. I see someone strong. Capable. Resilient.

And I know this journey wasn't just about remembering Marcus or building something new with him. It was about learning to love myself again—to believe in what I could do, even from a chair, even when my past was foggy.

Outside, I spot Marcus again, crouched next to a kid who looks like he's never caught a football in his life. He grins, encouraging the kid, demonstrating again, never impatient. That's the man I'm marrying. Not just the quarterback or the hometown golden boy—but the one who sees potential everywhere. Including in me.

My muscles ache, but I feel lighter than ever.

Later that afternoon, I'm sitting on our porch swing, sketchbook balanced on my lap, a half-drunk cup of peppermint tea beside me. I'm staying at his cabin for a few days. We are looking for a house to move into after we marry, but for now, these small adjustments will have to do.

Marcus is inside, rustling through papers and folders, probably buried in playbooks and outlines for the youth program he'll help run if he takes the coaching offer.

I listen to the sounds of him moving, the occasional thud of a binder hitting the table, and I smile. There's a peace in hearing someone you love just… exist in the next room. No need for constant words or attention—just the warmth of knowing they're near.

He steps outside a minute later, looking like a guy caught between excitement and chaos. His hair's slightly mussed, his shirt untucked, and he's holding what appears to be a very aggressive to-do list.

"You look like a man spiraling," I tease, flipping a page in my sketchbook.

Marcus groans, dropping onto the swing beside me. "I have no idea how one coaching gig comes with this much paperwork. I thought football was supposed to be about yelling at kids and drawing arrows."

I grin. "Turns out coaching's more than snacks and shouting. Who knew?"

He chuckles, leaning back and glancing sideways at me. "You good from therapy?"

I nod, bumping his knee with mine. "Crushed it. Samantha's threatening me with celebratory smoothies."

"That's my girl," he says, pride flickering in his eyes.

I set my pencil down and turn to him fully. "So… what's the latest on the job?"

He sighs, rubbing his neck. "Still deciding. It's everything I ever wanted—just… in a city four hours away."

I watch him carefully, gauging his expression. "Do you want it, Marcus?"

His brows draw together, like he's not sure how to answer.

"I think I do," he finally says. "But I also want this. You. The life we're building. And I hate the idea of missing even a minute of it."

I take his hand in mine, squeezing gently. "We're not broken glass, Marcus. We're strong. You don't have to choose one dream over another. If this job feels right, we'll figure it out."

He looks at me like he's seeing me all over again. "You really mean that?"

"I wouldn't have said yes to your proposal if I didn't."

He lets out a breath, pulling me gently into his arms. "How did I get so lucky?"

I rest my head on his shoulder, eyes closed. "You didn't run this time."

We stay there for a while, rocking gently on the swing. We talk about weekend visits and late-night video calls. About my magazine and his new coaching role. About Fairhope and second chances.

And as the sun dips behind the trees, casting our porch in golden light, I realize something quietly profound:

Love isn't just about holding on tight—it's about letting each other grow, even if that means doing some of it apart. We're not a couple bound by fear anymore. We're a team grounded by trust.

We'll make it work. I know we will.

~

After dinner, Marcus and I walk—well, I roll, he walks—down the little dirt path behind the community center, where the town recently cleared space for a new garden. It's not much yet, just some planters, wood chips, and a promise... but I already love it.

The kind of love you have for things with potential.

He pushes me slowly along the uneven path, the wheels bumping gently over the gravel. Above us, the sky blushes in shades of dusky rose and sleepy lavender. The sun is clocking out, but the cicadas are just getting started.

Marcus looks around and whistles low. "It's wild how different this looks from a year ago. Remember the rusted-out bike someone chained to that fence?"

I laugh. "And the mattress. I used to joke that this place was haunted by old furniture."

He grins. "Now it looks like it might be haunted by an overachieving gardener and a Girl Scout troop."

I swat his arm. "Don't disrespect the Girl Scouts. They build empires on Thin Mints."

He holds his hands up in surrender, chuckling. "Noted."

We come to a little bench beside a half-finished raised bed. I wheel myself beside it, and we sit in silence for a while. Not the awkward kind. The good kind. The kind where everything that needs to be said has already been said, but your souls still like the sound of each other.

I look at him, the easy curve of his smile, the familiar

creases around his eyes that only show when he's truly happy.

"You know," I say, tucking a strand of hair behind my ear, "I used to think love was supposed to be overwhelming. All-consuming. The kind of thing that wrecks you and then rebuilds you."

He turns to me slowly, brows raised. "And now?"

"Now I think it's more like this," I whisper. "Soft, steady. The quiet kind of love that holds the weight of your dreams without breaking. The kind that doesn't ask you to shrink to fit into someone else's life."

He's silent for a beat, then says, "I hope I make you feel that way."

"You do," I say without hesitation.

He reaches over, threads his fingers through mine, and gently brings our joined hands to his lips. "Then we're on the right track."

I glance down at my ring, at the shimmer that still makes me catch my breath sometimes. "This place used to be forgotten. And now it's growing into something beautiful."

Marcus follows my gaze. "Just like us."

A breeze rustles the leaves around us, soft and sweet. It feels like the world is exhaling, just like I am.

And then—just as I'm about to suggest we come back here next week to help plant something—the familiar sound of our mailbox's rusty creak echoes from the house.

Marcus's head tilts toward the sound. "You expecting anything?"

"Nope," I say, shrugging. "Probably wedding flyers."

"Or more unsolicited brochures about vinyl siding," he jokes, standing up.

He jogs toward the porch, his silhouette golden in the last of the daylight. I roll behind him slowly, curiosity tugging at me.

He opens the mailbox and freezes for a moment. "Huh."

"What?"

"This... looks official."

He hands me a thick envelope—cream-colored, hand-addressed in deep green ink. There's no return address. No company name. Just my name... and Marcus's.

I glance up at him. "Did you sign us up for some secret club I should know about?"

He shakes his head, wide-eyed. "Not unless it involves free food."

The seal is wax, deep red, with a faint impression I can't quite make out.

My fingers tremble as I break it.

Inside is a letter—heavy paper, the kind that means business—and a gold-embossed heading at the top: *Southern Creatives Alliance.*

I blink.

Marcus leans over my shoulder, reading with me. Together, we scan the first few lines.

Dear Annabelle Dawson and Marcus Gray,

We are honored to inform you that your recent submission to the Fairhope Community Arts Initiative, including the early circulation of your magazine project and accompanying community sports program, has been selected for regional spotlight and funding consideration...

My heart stutters.

I keep reading.

"Your story of resilience, creativity, and enduring partnership has deeply moved our selection committee. We believe your voices will inspire many, and as such, would like to feature you both at our upcoming fall showcase... with an attached grant offer to support your joint ventures."

"Oh my God," I whisper. "Marcus..."

He crouches beside me, eyes wide and shining. "Babe. They want to feature *us.*"

I read the last line aloud, my voice trembling.

"Your story has inspired us. Let us help you inspire others."

I cover my mouth with my hand, overwhelmed.

Marcus is grinning, his voice hushed but thrilled. "This changes everything."

I nod slowly, emotions bubbling over. "This... this is our next beginning."

He looks up at me, and even in the low light, I can see the question forming in his eyes—the same one spinning through my head.

Do we stay in Fairhope and build something permanent... or do we take this opportunity, leap into something bigger, scarier, more incredible?

I don't know yet.

But what I do know is this:

Whatever path we take, it's going to be together.

And that's the only certainty I've ever needed.

HAPPILY EVER AFTER

Marcus

*I*t's a beautiful evening. An evening so perfect that you want to bottle it up in time and keep it forever.

The fire's low in the hearth, flickering in that lazy, comforting way. The scent of cinnamon still lingers in the air from the apple crumble Annabelle made earlier—and yes, I may have eaten most of it before it cooled, and yes, my tongue is still slightly burnt, and no, I have no regrets.

We bought this house a month back, shortly after our wedding, and it's better than anything I could have imagined. Domestic, homely bliss might not have been something on my bucket list back in my teenage years or when I went to the big city, but now I realize how absolutely wonderful it can be.

Annabelle is curled up on the couch beside me, a big knit blanket around her shoulders, her sketchbook propped against one knee. She's got her glasses on—only wears them at night—and her hair's pulled up in a messy knot that she's tried to tame twice already. I love how she doesn't even realize how effortlessly beautiful she looks in these quiet, unfiltered moments.

I glance at her hand as she flips a page, and the flicker of her wedding band catches the firelight. My own ring feels warm and familiar on my finger—still new in that "whoa, I'm someone's husband" kind of way, but already so right it's like it's always been there.

Being married to Annabelle isn't some wild, dramatic thing. It's soft. Like a favorite hoodie or the way sunlight filters through the trees after a storm. It's grounding, good. She's good.

And somehow, this whole life we've built together? It's *ours.* The kind of life that sneaks up on you while you're too busy falling in love to realize you're building something real.

She shifts slightly and leans into me without looking up. "You're staring."

I grin. "Guilty."

She hums, still sketching. "You thinking about that pie you inhaled earlier?"

"Maybe. But mostly just admiring my stunning wife."

She snorts. "Stunning wife currently drawing a cartoon dog in a superhero cape."

I peer over her shoulder. "Is that… is that a baguette in its mouth?"

"Obviously. He fights crime *and* hunger."

I chuckle and rest my chin on her shoulder. "You know, ten years ago, if someone told me I'd be sitting on a couch with a wife who draws heroic carbs and bakes life-changing desserts, I probably would've laughed."

"And now?" she asks, teasing, eyes flicking to mine.

"Now I know I hit the damn jackpot."

She softens, her lips curving into that gentle smile she only gives me when she's caught off guard by her own happiness. "You're getting good at this husband thing."

"I try," I say, brushing a kiss against her temple.

The mantel above the fireplace holds a few of our favorite photos: one from the wedding, where we're laughing mid-vow; one from a lakeside picnic, where she tried to push me into the water and nearly tipped herself over; and a black-and-white shot Ethan took when we weren't looking—me helping her adjust her scarf, her hand resting gently on my chest.

That one's my favorite. It says everything without needing a single word. There's also one with my Dad and Mr. Dawson. Dad and I are trying to rebuild our broken relationship. It's not perfect yet, but we're getting there.

Our little home still smells faintly of fresh paint, which, although not my favorite smell, is comforting because it signifies new beginnings. The furniture is a mix of hand-me-downs and late-night online orders. There's a chalk-board in the kitchen with a list that reads:

order wildflower seeds

fix porch step

picnic date this weekend?

Some nights, I still can't believe this is mine—*she's* mine.

This life we share didn't come easy. We earned it, every crooked step of the way.

But sitting here with her, wrapped in warmth, with nothing but soft music and the sound of her pencil moving across the page?

Yeah. This right here—this is everything I never knew I wanted.

And somehow, everything I always needed.

We're still wrapped up in each other on the couch, hours later, though the fire's starting to burn low and the dog—

yeah, we've got one now, a sleepy golden retriever named *Toby* who thinks he's a lap dog—is snoring under the coffee table. Annabelle's sketchbook has been abandoned, and I've got her tucked into my side, her head on my chest and our hands laced together.

Outside, the world's gone still. Just crickets, wind, and a few distant porch lights blinking through the trees. Inside, it's us. This quiet little universe we built with hope and grit and a hell of a lot of late-night heart-to-hearts.

She sighs, real soft, and then murmurs, "Do you ever think about prom night?"

I blink. That was not where I thought she was going with that.

"You mean the night you wore those ridiculous sparkly heels and made me slow dance to *Savage Garden* under the bleachers?"

She lets out a breath of a laugh. "God, yes. And you had way too much cologne on."

"I was seventeen and trying to be irresistible."

"You smelled like a department store."

"I distinctly remember you saying I smelled 'intox-icating.'"

"I was trying to be polite," she deadpans, nudging me with her elbow.

We both dissolve into laughter, the kind that feels like exhaling years of old tension.

"I remember being terrified that night," I admit once we settle back into the quiet.

She looks up. "Of what?"

"Of messing everything up. Of not being enough for you. You always felt so... untouchable to me. Like the world already had plans for you, and I was just this guy trying to make varsity and get out of town."

Her eyes soften, and she traces a slow circle on my chest with her fingertip. "Marcus, I thought *you* were untouchable. Everyone adored you. You walked down the hall like the world was yours."

"Confidence," I say with a shrug, "was the mask. You were the only person I ever wanted to see through it."

She kisses my collarbone, then murmurs, "I'm glad we both took it off eventually."

"Me too."

We fall quiet again, and for a moment, I just let the peace of her weight against me fill up every corner of my soul. It's not always fireworks, this kind of love. Most days, it's softer—like the light at sunrise or the warmth of shared silence. But damn, it runs deep.

She shifts slightly and says, "We've come so far, haven't we?"

"Yeah," I nod, emotion tugging at my throat. "From hospital rooms and memory loss to wedding rings and community grants."

She smiles, glowing even in the dim firelight. "And Toby."

"Oh, obviously. He's the real glue holding this marriage together."

She swats my chest, giggling. "Don't tell him that. He already thinks he's royalty."

"He's not wrong," I say, looking toward the lump under the table. "But seriously, babe... I think about it all the time. How close we came to missing this. How different everything could've been if either of us had given up."

She's quiet for a beat, then says, "I think about that too. But I also think... maybe we were always meant to come back around. It just took the hard stuff to get here."

I pull her closer, press my lips to her temple. "You make all of it worth it."

There's a pause. Not heavy. Just thoughtful.

Then she says, "Do you ever think about the future? I mean—*really* think about it?"

I glance down. "All the time."

She shifts so she's looking at me, really looking. "I've been thinking lately about fostering."

I blink, surprised—but not in a bad way. "Yeah?"

She nods slowly. "I'm not saying tomorrow. But someday. There's room in this house. There's love. And... I don't know. I think I want to share it."

I don't respond right away because my heart's too full.

Finally, I manage, "You'd be amazing."

Her eyes glisten a little. "You think?"

"I *know*. And I'd be honored to do it with you."

She leans forward, kisses me slow and certain. "I love you, Marcus."

I kiss her back with every ounce of gratitude I have. "I love you more than I've ever loved anything in my life."

We rest our foreheads together for a long while, just breathing each other in.

The fire pops softly behind us.

And in this quiet, this peace, this stillness full of love and laughter and plans not yet fully formed—I know we've only just begun.

The fire's mostly embers now, glowing low in the hearth like it's been listening in on our whole conversation, quietly nodding along.

Annabelle's legs are stretched over mine, our blanket tucked around us like a cocoon. Toby has finally surrendered to sleep entirely, belly-up and snoring softly, his paw twitching like he's chasing rabbits in his dreams. I wish I could bottle up the warmth of this moment and carry it in my pocket for the rest of my life.

Annabelle's tracing the edge of my wedding band with her fingertip, like she's still a little surprised it's real.

I catch her hand gently and kiss it. "You ever regret any of it?" I ask, even though I'm scared of the answer.

She gives me a look—the kind that says I'm being ridiculous, but also that she understands exactly why I asked. "Not one second," she says softly. "Even the hard stuff. Especially the hard stuff. It's what brought us here."

I nod slowly, letting her words settle. "You know, every version of my life—every version of *me*—led back to you. And if I had to do it all over again, every mistake, every detour... I'd still choose this life. I'd still choose *you*."

She smiles in that way that hits me in the chest—soft, slow, and full of forever. "Even the part where I forgot who you were?"

I grin, brushing a strand of hair from her face. "Especially that part. Because I got to fall in love with you twice."

That gets her. Her eyes glisten, but she's still smiling, and she leans in and kisses me like I'm the only home she's ever needed. It's not one of those fireworks-in-the-sky, breathless movie kisses. It's slower. Sweeter. Like a promise sealed in quiet flame.

We stay like that for a while, pressed together under the soft hum of firelight and memory.

When we finally pull apart, she rests her head on my shoulder and whispers, "We've still got so many dreams left."

I nod. "And now we've got the foundation to build them all."

Outside, the wind picks up, rustling through the trees like it's carrying all our hopes into the future. Our little chalkboard calendar in the kitchen still says *Picnic Plans?* But we both know that our life isn't about just planning picnics or checking boxes.

It's about showing up. Choosing each other every day.

The world doesn't need to see us to know we're strong.

But I hope one day, some kid we help foster, or someone flipping through an issue of *Fairhope Sketchbook*, feels the ripple of the love we started here.

I tighten my arm around Annabelle, kiss the top of her head, and close my eyes.

This is what forever feels like.

Not loud. Not perfect.

Just *real*.

And ours.

ALSO BY SAVANNA SHAY

A Cowboy's Unexpected Promise

Whispers In Magnolia